Three Blind Eyes

She stifled a gasp. The brass bedstead in which her father lay under shabby-looking blankets stood in a room that was stripped and empty . . . Clothes lay untidily on the bare boards of the floor, together with a tin wash-basin standing on an upturned packing crate with a crumpled towel beside it.

Lucy has always felt secure and loved in the big old house she lives in with her father, and his second-hand clothes shop seems to provide them with all they need. But then she discovers things are missing from the house—furniture, paintings, silverware, even carpets and curtains. What is going on? Suddenly, her whole comfortable world is turned upside-down and she has to work as a skivvy to keep herself and her father. And just when she thinks things can't get any worse, her father is arrested for murder and Lucy finds herself drawn into the sinister and dangerous underworld of the east end of London, forced to work for the villainous blind man known as 'the Duke'. How can she prove her father's innocence when her every move is watched? It seems that everywhere she goes, she and Tom, her only friend, are in ever more deadly danger.

Alison Prince was born in London and at 17 she won a scholarship to the Slade School of Art. She was Head of Art at a London comprehensive school until she married and had three children, when she started writing. At first it was journalism and then children's television, for which she wrote several series including *Trumpton*, and appeared on *Jackanory*. This led to a publisher proposing she write her first book and she has been writing ever since. She lived on a farm in Suffolk and then moved gradually northwards and now lives on the Isle of Arran, which she has known and loved since childhood. She has won the Guardian Children's Fiction Award and has been shortlisted for the Smarties Award. *Three Blind Eyes* is her second book for Oxford University Press. Her first, *Oranges and Murder*, won the Scottish Children's Book of the Year Award, 2002.

Three Blind Eyes

Other Oxford books by Alison Prince

Oranges and Murder

Three Blind Eyes

Alison Prince

OXFORD
UNIVERSITY PRESS

OXFORD
UNIVERSITY PRESS

Great Clarendon Street, Oxford OX2 6DP

Oxford University Press is a department of the University of Oxford.
It furthers the University's objective of excellence in research, scholarship,
and education by publishing worldwide in

Oxford New York

Auckland Bangkok Buenos Aires
Cape Town Chennai Dar es Salaam Delhi Hong Kong Istanbul
Karachi Kolkata Kuala Lumpur Madrid Melbourne Mexico City Mumbai
Nairobi São Paulo Shanghai Taipei Tokyo Toronto

Oxford is a registered trade mark of Oxford University Press
in the UK and in certain other countries

British Library Cataloguing in Publication Data available

ISBN 0 19 271902 5

1 3 5 7 9 10 8 6 4 2

Typeset by AFS Image Setters Ltd, Glasgow

Printed in Great Britain by
Mackays of Chatham Ltd, Chatham, Kent

1

Lucy sat by the fire and listened while her father played. The notes of the flute rippled through the lamp-lit room and she closed her eyes with a contented sigh. Everything was so comfortable and safe. With the heavy velvet curtains drawn and the windows closed, nobody would know that Vine Street was just outside, leading down to Pickle Herring Stairs and the wharves with all their smells and noise and rattling of barrels over cobbles.

It was quiet out there now except for occasional footsteps and the yowl of a cat. The warehouses were closed for the night and the ships lay silent on the river. This was the best time, Lucy thought, when she and Papa were on their own, warm and private.

There was a tap at the door. Lucy's father stopped playing and sighed. 'I know who that will be,' he said. With the flute still in his hand, he walked across the room, his feet quiet on the Turkey carpet, and opened the door. 'Yes, Albert?'

The man who stood twisting the cord of his dressing gown between his fingers had a drooping moustache that made him look perpetually mournful. 'Please excuse me, Mr Bellman,' he said. 'I hate to be a nuisance, but it's just—'

'—one of your headaches?' Jeremy Bellman said. He managed to sound sympathetic.

Albert put his fingers to his forehead. 'I am afraid so. I have this neuralgia, as you know. And the flute—' He cast a sad glance at the instrument. 'If we could just have a little rest from it?'

Lucy wondered if her father was for once going to refuse. She saw the irritated shake of his head—but he took a deep breath and said, 'Very well, Albert.'

'I'm most grateful.' Albert gave a little bow then shuffled away in his worn leather slippers.

Lucy's father came back to the fire and took the flute apart, packing its sections into their case.

'Papa,' said Lucy, 'couldn't you let the room upstairs to someone else? Someone who likes music?' She blushed at her impertinence in suggesting such a thing—it was none of her business. But her father didn't seem to mind.

'I've thought of it,' he admitted. 'But in every other way, my dear, Albert is the ideal tenant. He's out every day at his clerking, and when he's here he's quiet. Apart from the matter of the flute, you'd hardly know he existed.'

'Except for the kippers,' said Lucy. 'You can smell them all over the house.'

'Well, yes. But you can't throw a man out for cooking kippers. Or for not liking the flute, come to that. He pays his rent every Friday, I never have to remind him. And that's a great blessing.'

Lucy said no more. As her father settled into his armchair and picked up a book to read, she found herself slightly uneasy. Did they actually *need* Albert's rent-money? It was a worrying idea. She'd always thought letting a room meant just what it said—you let someone occupy a room you weren't using, and, of course, they gave you some money for the favour, but that was a kind of courtesy. The tenants had seemed like distant members of the family rather than part of a business deal. There had been others before Albert, but none of them had stayed long. Lucy had never asked why. She'd assumed that they

2

weren't particularly friendly, and the question of whether they paid their rent had never occurred to her. Papa's money came from the shop downstairs, didn't it? There was no reason to need anything else.

Secretly, Lucy found the shop a little embarrassing. It smelt so frowsty, and the people who came in to rake about among the second-hand clothes were somehow frightening, shabby and unwashed, haggling fiercely over every farthing. They often smelt worse than the garments they hauled out of the pile to hold up against themselves and which they then stole if they could. The girls at Lucy's school sniggered behind her back about the shop. Until Miss Martin scolded them about it, they held their noses when Lucy came near them and fanned themselves with their hands. It was so unfair. Anything she wore that came from the shop was always washed and ironed first, and Ada Clegg, their live-in servant, brought a can of hot water to Lucy's room every morning so she could wash herself all over.

The fire was burning low. Lucy glanced at her father, but he had retreated into the world of his book. She picked up the brass tongs and added some more lumps of coal to the glowing embers, glad to do this small service for him. The grandfather clock ticked slowly. Nobody could ask for a more peaceful home, she thought. Some of the other girls had fathers who owned big houses with liveried footmen and carriages drawn by fine horses, but from what she saw, they seemed remote and severe, not like Papa, who was always kind. Look how he put up with Ada, who was the most truculent of servants, and how he had rescued Tom and Finn from the workhouse.

Lucy smiled as she thought of the two boys. Tom, a year older than herself, was her best friend, far closer than any of the snooty girls at school. He worked in the shop and Finn, his little brother, did his best to help. He

3

couldn't do much because of the twisted leg that made him hobble on the toes of an incurved foot, but he was happy and willing. *They're my family*, Lucy thought, *them and Papa.*

There was only one thing missing. As she watched the small flames start to lick up round the new coal, Lucy wondered again about her dead mother, whom she had never known. Her hair had been fair, like Lucy's, Papa had said, and she was small and slim, barely reaching his shoulder. Lucy had always pictured her as a frail woman, easily swept away by the dangerous business of childbirth. So sad for Papa, to lose his young wife and be left with a baby girl to bring up on his own.

But I'm twelve *now*, she thought. *Nearly thirteen. And then I'll put my hair up and wear long skirts. I'll be a woman.* Miss Martin had told her about that. Lucy's thoughts wandered on. *Perhaps Papa will think of me as more grown-up when I'm thirteen.* He had always been gentle and sweet, but when he sat frowning over private worries, he would never tell her what caused them, any more than he would explain where he went in the evenings. So often, he would leave the house 'to see friends' and return late, long after Lucy was in bed, but these visits seldom seemed to make him happy. Just occasionally, he would be laughing and triumphant at breakfast, talking of having had 'a good night', and then he would buy Lucy a present and be cheerful for several days—but more often he was cast down and anxious.

She looked at her father now, absently twining a strand of his thinning hair round his finger as he read, and smiled. *Dear Papa.* He was entitled to his small mysteries. Whatever they were, they could not disturb the trust she felt in him or the tranquillity of their life together. She picked up her own book, *Gulliver's Travels*, from where it lay on the floor, and began to read.

4

*   *   *

Quite early on the next Saturday morning, there was a loud banging at the front door. Lucy, coming down the stairs from the first-floor sitting-room above the shop, saw little Finn hurry across the hall with his lurching gait. He reached the door and opened it, and the large, straw-hatted man who stood on the step towered above him. 'Where's Mr Bellman?' the man asked.

Lucy recognized Harris, the butcher who supplied the household with meat. 'My father is out,' she said. 'Can I help you?'

'Give him this,' said the butcher. With a fist the size of a leg of lamb he thrust a folded paper into Lucy's hand. 'And tell him it's gone on long enough. If he doesn't settle up, I'll take action. And I'm not the only one. Good day to you.' And he turned and walked off.

Finn looked up, puzzled. 'What did he mean?' he asked.

Lucy scanned the list of black-pencilled items, and her face flamed. 'Nothing important,' she told the little boy. 'Off you go, back to the shop. Is Tom there?'

'Yes.'

Finn disappeared through the door that led from the hall into the rear of the shop, and Lucy stared again at the grease-blotched paper. The list was a long one. *Pork chops, beef topside, stewing lamb, sausages, minced beef, ham* . . . Each item was priced and dated, and the total was seven pounds, nine shillings, and eightpence. Under it, the butcher had written in heavy capitals, OWING AND OVERDUE.

Lucy's heart thudded with shock. She very much wanted to push the paper into the kitchen stove and burn the very thought of it away—but the butcher would only come back. He'd be there on the doorstep again in his bloodstained apron and straw hat, the sleeves of his black coat rolled back to show the dark hairs on his forearms, demanding his money in a voice loud enough for everyone in the street to hear.

Papa must have forgotten, she told herself. It was just some silly mistake. She went slowly up the stairs. Her father was not out as she had said—he'd come home very late last night and had not appeared at breakfast. She paused outside the door of his room, wondering what to do. It was his private sanctum, and she would never dream of disturbing him in there—but perhaps he ought to know about this.

If he doesn't settle up, I'll take action.

What did the butcher mean, *take action*? Lucy thought of his meaty hand bringing down a cleaver to crack through bone and sinew, and felt very scared. In the streets, so people said, a sailor might be found with his throat cut, lying among the cabbage stalks of the market on a grey morning, but the curtained windows had kept that rough, alarming world shut out. Whatever happened out there had nothing to do with the comfortable life lived within Papa's house. But now a part of it had come bursting in, and she didn't know what to do. Lucy tapped at her father's bedroom door.

There was no answer. She listened intently, but could hear no sound of movement. The brass can of hot water still stood outside, cold now. Very quietly, she turned the knob and pushed the door open a crack, and looked in.

She stifled a gasp. The brass bedstead in which her father lay under shabby-looking blankets stood in a room that was stripped and empty. Daylight beat in through curtainless windows, showing rectangles of unfaded wallpaper where pictures had been taken down. Clothes lay untidily on the bare boards of the floor, together with a tin wash-basin standing on an upturned packing crate with a crumpled towel beside it.

Lucy felt as if her joints had turned to water. She pulled the door closed again, quietly, quietly, terrified that her father would wake and know what she had seen. Then she ran to her own room, still crowded with the pretty things of her childhood, and flung herself on her bed, too numbed with shock to weep.

All this time, Papa had let her go to school every day, wearing polished boots and a coat that passed as quite smart, escorted by Ada who carried her little bag containing pens and sharpened pencils and the proper books. And he had been paring his own life down, selling things—yes, she was sure he must have been selling things—in order to try to meet the butcher's bill. How many other bills were there? How many more men were going to come to the door, threatening 'action'?

A grim curiosity made her roll over and bring her feet to the floor. Did Tom know what was going on? Did Ada know? Yes, almost certainly. Ada would have seen the tell-tale room; she'd have known the awful truth which Papa had tried to keep hidden. Oh, the shame of it! As if walking in a bad dream, Lucy made her way down the stairs and through the door to the shop.

Tom looked up from where he was watching two women turning over a pile of second-hand blouses, and smiled. 'Hello!' he said, sounding surprised. Lucy didn't often come into the shop.

She smiled back at him. They couldn't talk with the women there. She slipped behind the rows of coats and dresses hanging on rails to where household goods stood piled on tables, and hunted through them with a dreadful compulsion. Almost at once, she found the gilt-framed watercolour of cattle by a stream that used to hang above her father's bed. Sifting further, she unearthed his soap-dish, buried under other junk. There was no mistaking it—she had admired its pink shell with the gilt rim since her earliest years. There was nothing else on the tables as far as she could see, but among the jackets crammed together on hangers she spotted the embroidered waistcoat which Grandma had given her father for his birthday two years ago. She began to cry.

The women went out and Tom came to find her. 'Lucy! What's wrong? What's happened?'

She couldn't speak. Tom offered her a rather grubby hanky, and she blew her nose, struggling for words. He watched her in concern from under the shock of dark hair that came almost to his eyebrows. His grey eyes were worried.

'It's Papa,' she managed to blurt out.

'Is he ill?' Tom sounded alarmed. 'Shall I go for the doctor?'

'No.' Lucy put out her hand to touch the embroidered waistcoat. 'He's—oh, Tom, he's been selling everything. His room's empty. And the butcher came with a bill. He said he's not the only one.'

Tom was looking away, frowning in embarrassment.

Lucy stared at him. 'You knew,' she said.

He shrugged. 'Not really. Not about the butcher and everything.'

'Then what? *What* did you know?' Anger swept through her at the thought that she was the only one kept in the dark, protected from the truth like some china doll that might fall to pieces if subjected to any roughness.

'It's just—well, I haven't been paid for quite a while, so I knew things were difficult. It's all right,' Tom added quickly, 'I mean, I get my food and keep and so does Finn, and I don't expect any more, it was just a bit of pocket money for helping in the shop.'

'What about Ada?' Lucy demanded. 'Has she been paid?'

8

Tom frowned and his face reddened a little as he turned away to straighten the hangers. It was all the answer Lucy needed. 'You should have told me,' she said.

'He didn't want you to know,' said Tom.

No, of course not. A few moments went by while the awful truth sank in. She was the only thing left for Papa to feel proud of. While everything else crumbled away, she went on going to Miss Martin's Academy for Young Ladies, properly escorted by a servant and wearing her white gloves. 'But I thought the shop made money,' she said.

Tom didn't answer. He was turning over a cracked sugar bowl as if it was suddenly interesting, and his frown had deepened. Lucy put her hand on his rolled-up shirtsleeve. 'There's something else, isn't there?' she said. 'Tell me.'

Tom shook his head. 'It's not my business.'

They stared at each other, both of them wretched and determined—then the bell above the shop door tinged and a woman came in with a baby in her arms and several children round her. Tom turned away to attend to her. Customers could never be left unwatched, Lucy knew, specially when they had children with them. Among the very poor, thieving was a necessary part of the struggle to survive, and small fingers learned early how to make a quick, unseen grab.

She touched the embroidered waistcoat once again, longing to carry it back to her father's empty bedroom. But she could not. She knew the truth now, or at least part of it, and everything had changed. And what was the other secret, so shameful that Tom could not tell her? The illusion of safety had vanished like a forgotten dream, and she felt very alone. Slowly, she went back up the stairs to her room.

2

Lucy took the butcher's bill down to the front door and left it on the mat, as if it had just fallen through the letterbox. Then she turned and hurried away from it, almost running, in case Ada should come out of the kitchen and catch her putting it there.

She hated Ada. She hated her square, red face and the mouth kept shut because of the bad teeth inside it, and the way she sighed and puffed as if every task was too much for her, even though she had strong, brawny arms and tough fingers. Lucy remembered those fingers from the time when the last nanny had left and Ada was supposed to brush Lucy's hair and put it in curling papers each night. She had tugged so viciously that it brought tears to Lucy's eyes and taught her to manage her own hair. 'And so you should, young miss,' Ada had said. 'I've got enough to do.'

Curled up on the window seat in the chilly sitting room where the fire had not been lit, Lucy tried to read, but could not concentrate. She was listening with prickling attention for sounds of her father getting up, and when at last she heard his door open, she prayed that he'd go straight downstairs rather than come in here. She would never be able to meet his eye for the thought of the bill waiting to be found, and he'd know at once that there was something wrong.

She heard him go downstairs, and was thrown into fresh dread. He would come up here with the butcher's greasy paper in his hand, and she'd have to pretend it was a surprise to her. Lucy had never lied to her father—there had never been any temptation to do so, as he was always kind and understanding. She trusted him absolutely. But he hadn't trusted her—at least, not enough to share his worries. He loved her, there was no doubt of that, but she knew now that he didn't think of her as a responsible person with an opinion of her own. *My pet lamb*, he so often called her. *My darling*. A small piece of perfection that he wanted to keep undamaged.

But I'm not perfection, Lucy thought with a flare of sudden anger. *Why should I be? Doesn't everyone have a right to be a bit imperfect?*

He was coming upstairs. Lucy hunched herself more closely over her book. Outside, the sounds of the street drifted up from below—the talk and shouting, the scrape and clop of horses' hooves over cobblestones and the rumble of laden drays. Her father opened the door and came in, carrying a cup of coffee.

'Good morning, my darling.' He sounded easy and natural as he came across to join her on the window seat. He stirred his coffee and sipped it. 'I've been thinking—it's some time since we went down to Penge to see your grandma and grandpa. We might take a little trip, perhaps. Would you like that?'

'Oh, yes!' Lucy was startled out of her fears. Everything must be all right, after all, if he could afford a journey to see her beloved grandparents. The thought of his empty bedroom and the things for sale in the shop nagged at her, but she pushed them aside. Papa was not upset, he knew what he was doing. 'When can we go?' she asked.

Jeremy smiled at his daughter's eager face. 'Tomorrow,' he said. 'First thing.'

It was barely dawn when they set out. Lucy had a basket

11

containing a few things of her own and some bread and cheese and a bottle of lemonade for the journey, and her father carried a rug and a leather travelling bag. There was an orange streak in the sky above the houses, but everything was grey and still. The ships lay silent in the river with no wind to rattle their ropes and rigging, and nothing moved in the streets except the occasional scurry of a rat. Lucy clutched her coat round her when she saw the first of the quick-moving creatures, afraid it might come swarming up her black-stockinged legs, but her father laughed.

'Rats won't hurt you,' he said. 'They're like us, they only want to stay alive and feed their families. And where would we be without them? They eat up a lot of the rubbish.'

'But they're horrible,' Lucy objected.

'So are many things, my pet lamb.' Jeremy patted Lucy's hand that was looped through his arm. 'But they may be useful, all the same.'

He said no more, and she wondered what he had meant. *So are many things.* Small questions were at work in her mind now that had never troubled her before. Her father had become mysterious. She hugged his arm a little more tightly as they walked through the lanes and alleys of Southwark, glad to be with him despite all the puzzles, and the dawn light gradually grew stronger.

They came out into a broad road that went over London Bridge. Most of the traffic was heading that way, into the city. A small group of bullocks ambled along, guided by a man and two small boys and a dog, and the cab driver behind them cracked his whip impatiently, urging his horse past them. He nearly collided with a costermonger's barrow coming the other way, laden with apples and vegetables, and the coster halted his donkey and yelled, 'Where d'you think you're going?' An omnibus behind the cab had to stop, and a general shouting match broke out.

'They're all in such a hurry,' said Lucy.

'All desperate to make a bit of money,' her father agreed. 'Sell their vegetables, get on with their business, be at their offices to start work.'

'And we're just going on a holiday,' Lucy said happily. 'Aren't we lucky?'

'Yes, indeed,' said Jeremy. But when she glanced up at him, she saw that he was not smiling.

In the next moment, the coach came over the bridge, and it was such a marvellous sight that Lucy forgot her concerns. 'Oh, Papa, look!' The four horses were striding out, fresh and eager, and the coachman sat on his box like a king on his throne, the reins in one hand and his long whip in the other, proof against all weathers in his heavy coat with its three layers of cape on the shoulders.

He reined in the horses and hauled up the brake of the carriage, and the heavy vehicle came to a stop beside them. 'No room inside,' he shouted down. 'On top only. Where are you going?'

'Dulwich—all the way.' Jeremy reached up to hand the driver some money.

'Right—up you get.'

Lucy scrambled up the iron rungs of the ladder on the side of the coach, her father following. A woman wrapped in several shawls moved along the bench seat to make room, and the driver set off again with a crack of his whip.

It seemed terribly high up, Lucy thought. And what was there to stop you falling off except the narrow brass rail? She didn't remember feeling so high-perched before, but it was a long time since their last trip. She had been smaller then, and more safely sandwiched between grown-up people. Her father tucked the rug round their

13

knees, and Lucy was glad of it, for the speed of the horses made it windy up here, and she was already feeling chilled.

They went through Walworth and made a stop in Camberwell, where a couple of the inside passengers got out. Lucy looked down at them from her high perch—a man in a coat with an astrakhan collar and a woman carrying a little dog—and wondered if her father would suggest moving down to occupy the inside seats, but he said, 'Stuffy in there.'

'And double the price,' put in the woman next to them.

The coachman blew his horn, and they were off again. When they came to the long slope of Dulwich Hill, he halted and yelled, 'All outside passengers off!' Everyone obediently climbed down the ladder. Lucy remembered this from previous visits, walking up the hill beside the labouring horses. It had been raining last time, and one of them had slipped and almost fallen. Today, she didn't mind the walk, for the day was dry and crisp. Besides, her hands and feet were cold, and the exercise would warm her up.

At the top, they were allowed on again.

'Where's that bread and cheese?' Jeremy asked. 'I'm ravenous.'

Lucy got the supplies out of her basket, and the sun beamed out as they rattled along, munching happily. The city smells of beer and stinking drains and food frying were left behind now, and the air was full of freshness, with sometimes a waft of woodsmoke and autumn leaves or the heady scent of fallen, fermenting apples. The coach clattered into an inn yard in the pretty village of Dulwich, and among a great bustle of disembarking, ostlers came out to unharness the steaming horses and lead them away to the stables.

Now for the walk, Lucy thought with pleasure. This was the perfect day for it, with the sun shining in a September sky that was as blue as the Michaelmas daisies in the cottage gardens. She and her father climbed the hill on the further side of Dulwich, and at the top they came to the signpost where the roads divided.

'Penge Common.' She read the words aloud, remembering the stretch of grassy land, rich with buttercups and cow parsley, and the stream where she had dabbled her hands and scooped up the clear water to drink. There was a gate now where all traffic had to stop and pay a toll, but the woman in charge let the pair of them through for nothing, as they were on foot. A black-painted notice behind her gave a stern warning. ALL TRESPASSERS ON THESE WOODS WILL BE PROSECUTED, AND THE CONSTABLES HAVE ORDERS TO TAKE THEM INTO CUSTODY.

The words chilled Lucy despite the warmth of the autumn day. *Take them into custody.* That meant, arrested. Thrown into prison. As a child, she had thought it was only children who were punished for disobedience, but she saw now that it applied to grown-up people as well. Nobody was quite free. You had to obey the rules, even if you didn't understand them.

'This land used to be open to everyone,' her father said as they walked on, 'until the owner of the big estate declared it his. There were cottages here, each with its own garden that grew enough for its occupants to live on. They grazed their cows on the common and reared a pig each year to see them through the winter. All gone now. Cleared away.'

'But where to?' asked Lucy. 'Where did the people go?'

'The workhouse, I suppose. But why spoil our day with sad thoughts?' her father added. 'Look over there— blackberries!'

The bushes had been well picked over, but there were good clusters still to be had.

'I wish we lived in the country,' Lucy said as they went on their way with stained fingers and mouths.

'Do you, my darling?' Jeremy gazed up at the elm trees where rooks were assembling with a rumpus of untidy cawing. 'Well, perhaps we will one day, with luck. But the city is the place for luck, Lucy. Fortunes can be made there.'

'Can they?' She looked at him with fresh interest. 'Will you make a fortune, Papa?'

'Oh, yes,' said her father, and laughed with the dizzy certainty of it. 'I'm going to make a fortune, pet lamb, you can be sure of that.'

'Will it happen soon?' asked Lucy.

'It might do.' His head was up and he was smiling as he walked. 'Any day now, my luck will turn. The thing is to keep giving it a chance, that's all.'

'I see,' said Lucy. And wished she did.

The sun was low in the sky by the time they came to the Old Crooked Billet, but its red glow reflected warmly from the windows of the inn. A big willow tree half hid its weathered pantiles, and beyond this a path led round to the stables and the barn. A woman was coming along it with a basket over her arm, and Lucy ran to meet her.

'Grandma!'

'Lucy! Heavens! And how you've grown! Why didn't you let us know you were coming?' Lucy was being hugged as nobody had hugged her since the last time she was here, and the basket of fresh brown eggs almost spilled.

Her grandfather had come out of the inn and was approaching them, broader and stouter than she

16

remembered him, with his sleeves rolled up and a striped apron tied round his middle. He kissed Lucy, then looked at her father.

'Well, Jeremy.' It wasn't a greeting exactly, but something more like a question. 'You'd better come in.'

Perhaps they should not have arrived without writing first, Lucy thought. She worried about it a little as they all went into the taproom where three or four men were sitting round the fire with mugs of ale—but her grandfather did not seem seriously displeased. 'You'll be hungry after such a journey,' he said.

'There's plenty of cold beef and we've carrots and potatoes from the garden.' Lucy's grandmother was full of welcome. 'And I made a batch of bread this morning. Come along upstairs—we've only two couples staying just now, so there's plenty of space.'

Lucy remembered the little room with its sloping ceiling and flowered curtains at the window that looked out over the fields. 'Oh, Grandma, it's so nice to be here,' she said.

'Nice for us, too, my pet. It's been too long. There's water in the jug if you want to wash your hands. Just come down when you're ready.'

The other guests ate with them round the big table, and Lucy's grandfather served them with mugs of ale from the barrels that stood on trestles by the wall. The ladies had small glasses of elderflower wine, and one of them nodded appreciatively. 'This is very good, Mrs Ash.'

'The trees bloomed well this year,' Lucy's grandmother said modestly. 'Lucy, are you old enough to try a little drop, with some water?'

'May I, Papa?'

'Why not?' said her father, wiping beer froth from his moustache. 'You're growing up, I suppose. I'll have to get used to it.'

The wine was so fragrant that it seemed as if the bush with its creamy flowers was blossoming again in the very room, but the taste was clean and sugarless. 'It's lovely,' Lucy said, and her grandmother gave her a little more.

When the meal was over and the dishes were cleared from the table, Lucy's grandfather asked, 'Did you bring your flute, Jeremy? You could give us a tune.'

'I did, as it happens.' Jeremy took the flute in its case from the leather travelling bag, put it together and played a preliminary flourish, then started on a merry jig that had everyone tapping their feet. One tune led to another, and everyone joined in singing the words of the old songs, 'Barbara Allen', 'Greensleeves', 'Drink to me Only with thine Eyes'. Then he played 'Shepherds' Hey', and the two couples got up to dance. Their shadows leapt on the wall, and Lucy suddenly found that her eyes were closing. She tried to blink them awake, but her grandmother said, 'You've had a long day, sweetheart. I'll light you a candle.'

Lucy followed her up the narrow wooden stairs to her room, and her grandmother said, 'You won't want me to tuck you in now you're a big girl.'

Lucy wouldn't have minded being tucked in, but she smiled and shook her head. After all, she was nearly thirteen. Her grandmother kissed her and said, 'God keep you safe through the night.'

'Amen,' said Lucy dutifully.

'Don't forget to blow your candle out.'

'I won't,' Lucy promised.

Alone in the little room, she changed quickly into her nightdress and got into the bed with its quilted cover. *God keep you safe through the night.* It was what Grandma had always said, even when Lucy was small. As if the night was full of hidden dangers. But then, Grandma's daughter, the girl who had become Lucy's mother, had died, perhaps

18

during some terrible night, a few hours after she had given birth to Lucy. Maybe as people got older, they learned that there were things to fear. But here, in this warm, welcoming house, there could be no threats. Lucy blew her candle out and slept.

3

The next morning, the room felt sharply cold, though Lucy was warm under the soft covers. She sat up and pulled the curtains back from the little window, and saw that frost lay white on the rows of cabbages in the garden and powdered the grass where the sun had not reached it.

Downstairs in the kitchen, the iron door of the bread oven was hot to the touch. There was no sign of her grandmother, but she could hear wood being chopped outside, and went out to find her grandfather splitting logs for kindling.

'There you are—did you sleep well?' he asked.

'Yes, thank you.' Lucy wondered what time it was. She suspected that her grandparents had been up for hours, though the yellow sun was only just above the apple trees.

'Had your breakfast?' Her grandfather brought the axe down again, and the log fell into two halves. He stooped to pick one of them up to cut again. 'Your grandma's in the garden,' he added, not waiting for an answer.

'I'll go and see her.' Lucy had already spotted the shawled figure bending over rows of vegetables.

Her grandmother straightened up as she approached. 'Good morning, my dear.' She put a white, fat-stemmed leek on top of the others in the basket beside her. 'That'll be enough. Time to get the bread out of the oven. Are you hungry?'

Lucy hadn't thought about it, but she nodded. There

20

was nothing like fresh bread, with butter sliding off it because it was still hot. 'You must have been up very early,' she said.

'Half past five,' said her grandmother, sounding matter-of-fact. 'We'd never get everything done otherwise. I don't make bread every day, only if we've a houseful, but there's always the cow to be milked, and the pig and the chickens to be fed, and fires to be lit. Your grandpa sees to the horses—sometimes there are quite a few if we've a lot of people staying, and we often have orders to get them harnessed and ready for an early start.' She picked up the basket of leeks and handed them to Lucy. 'You carry those and I'll bring the fork.'

'Don't you get tired?' Lucy asked. 'It sounds like a lot of work.'

Her grandmother glanced at her as they crunched across the frosty grass. 'Never be afraid of work, Lucy,' she said. 'Children always think it's hard, because they aren't strong enough for it, but as you grow up, you find you can do more than you think. Come and meet my bees,' she added, leading the way between grey and leafless lavender bushes to where hives stood under the apple trees.

There wasn't a bee to be seen. 'It's too cold for them to fly,' Lucy's grandmother explained, 'but they're in there. And they'll want to know you're here. You must always tell your family news to the bees, or they may fly away and leave you. This is Lucy,' she told the first hive. 'She's my granddaughter. You know her, don't you? She's here with her father.' She moved down the row of hives, stooping at each one to repeat her message, and the seriousness with which she spoke prevented Lucy from smiling. 'And now we'll fry some bacon for breakfast,' her grandmother ended.

This time, Lucy did smile. 'I never knew bees ate bacon,' she said.

21

'For you, you cuckoo! And your father. The bees are all right—I've left them plenty of honey to see them through the winter.'

Jeremy was up when they got back to the house, and they all sat down to rashers of bacon cut from the side that hung in the dairy, with eggs and fried potatoes, then hot bread spread with butter and honey, and fresh, creamy milk. Afterwards, Lucy wanted to help her grandmother wash the dishes, to show that she wasn't afraid of work, but it was going to take time to heat the water, and her father said they should be going, otherwise they'd miss the afternoon coach back to London.

'I thought we were staying longer,' Lucy said, disappointed.

'So did I,' said her grandmother. 'All this time, then you're only here for a few hours.'

'I'm sorry,' said Jeremy. 'It's just—I have business to attend to.'

And Lucy's grandmother said nothing.

The next morning, quite early, Jeremy handed Tom a sealed envelope and said, 'Run round to Harris the butcher for me, and give him this. And ask if we can have a leg of pork.'

'Can I go, too?' asked little Finn.

'No, your brother will be quicker on his own.' Then Jeremy added kindly, 'Besides, I want you to help me sort some new stuff for the shop.'

Tom didn't look at Lucy as he went out with the envelope pushed deep into his jacket pocket, but an understanding bridged the air between them. *This is the money to pay the bill.* Jeremy suddenly wasn't poor any more.

Ada was waiting to take Lucy to school. 'Are you

coming, young miss?' she enquired. 'I've more to do than stand about here all day.'

'Oh—yes, of course. I'm sorry.'

Ada had given up any pretence of being polite, Lucy thought as they set off through the streets together. Only a few days ago, when Papa had asked her if she could wash the gravy-stained tablecloth that hadn't been changed for days, she put her fists on her hips and said, 'If you're not satisfied, Mr Bellman, then get yourself another housekeeper.' And she had reason to be cross, Lucy thought, if she hadn't been paid.

Perhaps things were all right now. Maybe the fortune her father talked of had suddenly arrived, and all the difficulties were behind them. At breakfast, he had promised Lucy a new pair of boots to wear to school, and that would be good, because the old ones were so tight that they hurt her toes.

'So you've been to see your grandpa,' said Ada. She didn't often speak to Lucy on the way to school, so her comment came as a surprise.

'Yes. And Grandma.'

'Thought as much. Not a word to me, of course, just says you're off on a little trip. But I've seen it all before.'

Lucy sensed danger, but she didn't know how to avoid it. 'Seen what?' she asked reluctantly.

'Little trips down to Penge. Comes back the fine gentleman, doesn't he, money in his pocket, paying the bills, buying little presents. Not that it ever does me any good.'

Lucy felt her face burn crimson. She walked on, looking down at the shabby, outgrown boots that were going to be replaced, and wondered what to say. The silence lasted until they reached the school, and it hung about her for the rest of the day like a stray dog, eyeing her reproachfully. Perhaps she should have said something to

Ada about being sure Papa would pay her soon, but she was only twelve. Whatever she said would sound cheeky.

For the rest of the day, Lucy kept thinking of Ada's words. Twice during the lessons, Miss Martin had to reprove her for being inattentive, and at the end of the day she kept her back and asked, 'Is there anything wrong, my dear? It's not like you to be absent-minded.'

Lucy shook her head, but she was close to tears. Her memory of the lovely visit to Penge was ruined, and she felt humiliated by knowing now that she had simply enjoyed it like a child, never wondering about its purpose. If Papa had gone there just to borrow money, it made the whole thing seem so grubby. And what would happen when the money ran out and they were back to poverty?

Ada was standing in the doorway, waiting to fetch her home, and Lucy glanced at her uneasily.

Miss Martin understood. 'Lucy, I'm always here,' she said quietly. 'If there is anything you would like to discuss privately at any time, I am at your disposal.'

'Thank you,' Lucy whispered.

Ada was silent all the way home, but Lucy's thoughts continued in their turmoil. She knew now that her father kept a part of his life secret from her. He had borrowed money from Grandpa, that was obvious—but why? What was happening to the money from the shop? She'd always assumed it was enough for them to live on, but there was a doubt about that now. Maybe Papa had expenses she didn't know about. Tom had hinted at something of the kind. *It's not my business*, he'd said.

What can a man spend money on? Lucy wished she knew more about the world of grown-up people. There was drink, of course—but Papa didn't drink, except for an occasional glass of dark ale, which he said was good for him.

A lady friend. Lucy almost stumbled as this idea hit

her, and Ada said, 'Pick your feet up, stupid.' Was it possible? Papa was a good-looking man. His brown hair was thinning a little, but he had a nice smile under his curly moustache, with strong, white teeth, not like Ada's that were gappy and rotten. But if he had a friend, surely he'd bring her home?

A worse thought came. Some women, Lucy had heard, asked for money for the pleasure of their company. No, Papa wouldn't have anything to do with people like that, would he? But there was a secret of some sort.

As soon as they got home, Lucy went into the shop. Tom was on his own.

'Where's Papa?' she asked.

'He went out about an hour ago,' Tom said. 'He didn't say where.'

'And Finn?' Lucy wanted to be sure they wouldn't be overheard.

'He's upstairs. His leg's hurting him—it does sometimes.'

Lucy took a deep breath. 'Tom, listen, you've got to tell me. Something's happening to the money, isn't it? Something to do with Papa.'

Tom looked away, and Lucy rushed on, 'I'm not a child, I'm nearly as old as you. I want to know.'

'You'd best ask him yourself,' said Tom.

'I can't,' Lucy said. 'Not if it's—' No, she couldn't say it.

'Not if it's what?' Tom asked.

She blushed. 'Something's costing him a lot of money, I can see that. I've been trying to think what it could be. And I just thought . . . I just wondered . . . ' She was stammering in her embarrassment. 'I've heard there are women who have to be paid.'

'No!' Tom sounded shocked. 'He wouldn't, not in a thousand years.'

'Then what is it?' Lucy demanded. 'Tom, *please*!'

For a moment, he didn't answer, then his eyes met hers under frowning brows. 'It's not as bad as you think. He just gambles a bit, that's all.'

'Gambles?' It was a new word to her. 'What do you mean?'

'Betting. A card game or dice, something like that. All the players put in money, and the one who wins takes the lot.'

'But if you lose—'

'Well, you lose, that's all. Only some people always believe they're going to win, so they go on and on losing.' Tom put his hand on her sleeve. 'Lucy, don't look so upset. I'm sorry, I shouldn't have told you.'

'Yes, you *should*,' Lucy said fiercely. The truth fitted so neatly that it shocked her, but it brought a kind of satisfaction. 'I just wish I'd known before, that's all.' *I'm going to make a fortune, pet lamb*. If she'd understood, she could have told Papa not to worry about making a fortune, they were all right as they were.

Tom was watching her. 'The trouble is,' he said, 'he can't bear not to take the chance, in case he misses the big win. I've heard Ada's friends talking about it.'

'Yes,' said Lucy. But surely he could change? They could live as Grandpa and Grandma did, working hard and eating good food and enjoying music in the evening. Her grandparents made enough to live on, didn't they? Even enough to lend to other people. She thought of her grandfather's unsmiling face as they left the inn, and a new piece of understanding dropped sickeningly into place. Grandpa knew the money he had lent her father would never come back.

'Any hope of a cup of tea?' Tom asked. 'I didn't get off for a lunch-break today. Ada's supposed to come and mind the shop for half an hour, but sometimes she doesn't.'

'I'll go and get you one,' said Lucy.

Ada was not alone in the kitchen. A skinny boy crouched on a stool in the corner, and a big, craggy man in a black waistcoat was sitting on a chair by the stove, his feet spread out to its warmth. His greying hair emerged in lank curls from under the cap on the back of his head, and a stick leaned against the arm of his chair. He turned his head as Lucy came in—and she stifled a gasp. One of his eyes was sunken and half shut, and the other had red-rimmed lids that stretched over a bulging white ball with a pale blue centre, as dead as the stare of a china doll.

'Who's there?' he asked.

'Only Bellman's girl,' said Ada. 'What do you want?' she added to Lucy.

'A cup of tea for Tom, he's had nothing all day,' Lucy said bravely. 'I'll make it if you're busy.'

'No, you won't,' said Ada.

'I wouldn't mind a cup myself,' said the man with the glass eye. And Ada moved the kettle onto the hot part of the stove.

'Tom,' said Lucy, putting two cups of tea and a hunk of buttered bread on the shop counter, 'there's a blind man in the kitchen. He's got a glass eye.' There was a trader in the market who sold glass eyes, lots of them on a tray covered with green baize, blue ones and brown ones and grey ones. She'd always been horribly fascinated by the way they rolled about, gazing all ways.

'That's the Duke,' said Tom. 'Marmaduke Evans. Ada's friend.' He bit into the bread and chewed hungrily, then added, 'There's a lot of her friends come into the kitchen now, specially in the evenings. And a right lot of rogues they are.'

27

Lucy stared at him. 'Does Papa know?'

Tom shrugged and went on eating, and the truth was plain without words. Ada was often unpaid, so she didn't have to stay. If she chose to do so, Jeremy Bellman could hardly complain if she had her friends in. Lucy's fingers clasped the hot cup of tea, but its warmth did not dispel an ominous sense of chill.

Her father came home late that night, so late that Lucy hardly stirred in her sleep as she heard him go into his room. The next morning, he was silent and unsmiling at breakfast, leaning one elbow on the table with his head in his hand as he stirred his tea dispiritedly. Outside, the windows were white with the river fog that hung in the streets, and the creeping coldness of it penetrated into the dining room, where Ada had not lit the fire.

I should say something, Lucy thought, but no words would come. She thought uneasily of the money borrowed from her grandfather. Had all of it gone last night over the games of cards or dice?

Her father caught her looking at him, and gave her a thin smile. 'I've rather a headache, my dear,' he said.

Like Albert Apps, who had a headache when he wanted the flute to stop. *Papa wants the bad luck to stop*, Lucy thought. *He wants to be happy and take life easy*. And who could blame him? With sudden courage, she asked, 'Was it an unlucky night?'

Her father stared at her. He sat back in his chair and dabbed his mouth with his napkin. Then he said, 'What do you mean, exactly?'

The coldness of his tone was a shock. Floundering for words, Lucy said, 'When we were going to Penge—you said you might make a fortune, if you were lucky.' She knew her face was scarlet.

28

Jeremy did not smile. 'You have been gossiping,' he said. 'I am surprised at you, Lucy.'

'No, I haven't, I just thought—'

'My own daughter.' He tossed the napkin onto the table in front of him. It was crumpled and long unwashed.

'Papa, please!' Lucy was in tears.

Jeremy's anger dissolved as quickly as it had flared up. He pushed his chair back and came to stand beside her, cradling her head against his jacket. 'I'm sorry, my dear.' He was stroking her hair. 'I've tried so hard to keep you safe. I don't want these things to touch you.'

'But, Papa,' Lucy blurted, 'I'm growing up. I want to help you.'

'Then stay innocent, my love,' her father said. 'Give me something to believe in. Something in this life has to be good.' His hand stilled in its stroking, and for a moment he pressed her close to him. Then he turned and left the room.

The days that followed were like a bad dream. Lucy's father walked about with a drawn, anxious face, and more things found their way from the house to the shop. The clock went from the dining room mantelpiece, together with the mahogany plant-stand, complete with its aspidistra in the olive-green glazed pot. Pictures disappeared from the walls of the hall and the sitting room. Each morning, Lucy found the house looking thinner and more bare.

She did not mention the changes to her father, but she went often into the shop for a painful confirmation of what was being sold. Some things, however, didn't appear on the crowded trestle tables—the dining room clock, for instance, and the cut-glass inkwells from the desk in the sitting room—and, most distressing of all, the pin-cushion that had been Lucy's mother's. Lucy had loved it since she was small, because it was in the form of a silver chick emerging from its egg, with a dark velvet back where its fluff should be. These more valuable things had gone somewhere else—she couldn't guess where.

A day or two later on their way home from school, Ada paused to glance into the window of a poky shop with the sign of three golden balls above its door. There amid the other stuff was the silver pin-cushion.

Ada did not seem surprised. She gave a bark of laughter and said, 'Pawning things is a fool's game.'

Lucy was furious at being shown this so deliberately, but she tried to sound casual. 'Why is it?'

'Every pound they lend you, they want a pound and four shillings back,' said Ada.

Dry-mouthed, Lucy asked, 'And if you can't pay it?'

'After a year, they can sell it. Look at their shops, crammed with stuff. Fools,' Ada said again, with contempt, then set off again down the cobbled street, not waiting to see if Lucy was following.

Out of the same awful curiosity that drove her into the shop, Lucy started finding reasons to go more often into the kitchen. Tom was right—there were often strange people in there, warming their hands by the stove or sitting at the table with a jug of beer brought in from the ale-house along the street. The blind man called the Duke was almost always there, together with the skinny boy who acted as his guide, but there were others as well, a weasel-faced lad with red hair, and several raucous women, and a man they called Slip. He was as thin and quick-moving as an alley cat, and his nose had a deep groove across it, blue and discoloured, as though dirt and crushed bone had been forced into the dented skin.

30

Ada's friends mostly ignored Lucy, though sometimes their conversation would stop abruptly when she came into the room. She took to listening for a moment before she opened the door, and if the voices were low and muttered, she went away again in case something private was being discussed. Once, as she came to the door, she heard Ada laugh and say, 'Old Bellman can't last much longer. Then we'll see, won't we?' There was a cackle of amusement and mugs were thumped on the table, and Lucy fled.

One morning about a week later, Jeremy opened an official-looking letter at breakfast, then sat back in dismay. 'Oh, dear, dear,' he said, scanning the page again as if he couldn't believe what it told him.

Lucy put her piece of bread down. 'Papa, what is it?'

Her father got to his feet and stared out of the window into the yard, though she knew there was nothing to see out there but the washing line and the roof of the privy. Then he turned back to Lucy. 'My darling, there is sad news, I'm afraid,' he said. 'Your grandfather died three days ago.'

'Grandpa?' She could barely whisper the word. Tears stung in her eyes. 'But how?' He was so strong. So solid, with his apron tied round his middle.

'An accident, it seems. I don't know any details. This is from the lawyers.' He sat down again and glanced at a couple more letters, then tore one of them open and read it. Lucy recognized her grandmother's writing, and waited in dread to hear what the neat lines said. Her father's voice went on.

'Some stupid young man driving a phaeton and pair much too fast along the lane that leads to Croydon. A wheel came off in a rut, threw the thing sideways. Your

31

grandfather was coming the other way in the dog-cart, took the full force of it. His neck was broken. The horse had to be shot.' Jeremy's voice wobbled a little. He took his handkerchief from his pocket and blew his nose. 'I'll have to go down there,' he said. 'At once.'

4

There was no joy in this visit. The house was full of hushed people in dark clothes, and Lucy's grandmother seemed shrunken and aged by the shock. On the morning of the funeral, the church was packed with villagers, but outside, cold rain blew across the common, and the mourners who stood among the gravestones to watch the coffin being lowered into the ground had their shoulders hunched against the driving wetness.

After the lunch of cold ham and rabbit pie, Lucy felt purposeless. She did not belong among the hushed relatives who sat in the parlour with her grandmother, listening to what the solicitor from London had to say, but neither was she part of the busy group of local women who washed dishes and threw scraps out for the hens in the yard. Annie, the girl who worked as a barmaid in the inn, took pity on her.

'Help me fold these tablecloths, Lucy,' she said, though there were plenty of other people who could have done it. She chattered as they brushed off crumbs and folded the white linen, bundling any stained cloths into the washing basket. 'I'll miss your grandpa—such a nice gentleman, you couldn't ask for a better. And your grandma, too. The place won't be the same without them.'

'But Grandma will still be here,' Lucy said.

Annie shook her head. 'She could never manage it alone. And Mr Ash was a tenant. The landlords will want

33

a younger couple, I expect.' She looked at Lucy hopefully. 'You haven't heard what's to happen?'

'No,' said Lucy.

Annie was disappointed. 'I don't know if I'll still have my job,' she said. 'I thought you might know.'

'I'm sorry,' said Lucy. So that was why Annie had spoken to her—not out of sympathy, but just because she was hoping for news.

When all the tables were cleared, Lucy slipped into the garden. The rain had stopped, but the grass was still wet underfoot, and the fading daylight was heavy with cloud. She made her way to the rows of beehives under the apple trees, and stared at them. Did the colonies inside them really want to know what was happening to the people of the house? Could they really care? She hoped they could, because she felt very alone.

'Grandma may be going away,' she told the unseen bees. 'I don't know what's going to happen. Please take care of her.'

She stared at the silent hives for a few moments longer, then turned to go back to the house—and saw her grandmother coming over the grass, clutching a grey shawl round her head and shoulders. Neither of them spoke until they were close, and then Lucy found herself enveloped in arms and shawl, pressed close with surprising strength.

'You were talking to the bees,' her grandmother said when she released her.

'Yes.' After a pause, Lucy asked, 'Are you going to leave here?'

'Yes, darling. I have to. I'd thought of trying to keep the inn going, with a hired man to do the heavy work, but it wouldn't be the same. And the landlord wants a new couple. I can't blame him.'

'But where will you go?'

'To my sister-in-law, Cathie. Your great-aunt. She's here, you've met her.'

'Yes.' Great-Aunt Cathie was a fat woman with a hairy chin. 'Where does she live?'

'In Exeter. She's been widowed for some years, she'll enjoy the company.'

'Where's Exeter?'

'Down in the West Country. A long way from here, I'm afraid.'

Lucy nodded, trying to be brave. *Exeter*. It sounded like *exit*. Go out, go away. The Latin learned with Miss Martin suddenly had a new, very real meaning. *Exeunt*, all go out, like the end of a Shakespeare scene when the stage emptied. 'I'll never see you,' she said bleakly. Even to get from London to Penge took most of the day, and how much further was it to the place called Exeter? What would it cost?

'We'll find a way,' said her grandmother. 'There are these wonderful railways now. Wouldn't it be exciting, to go on a train?'

'Yes,' said Lucy. She knew it was only a dream, and knew she must not say so. 'It's getting cold,' she said.

The shawl was round her again, and they were walking back to the house.

One evening a few weeks after their return to London, Lucy was in the shop talking to Tom when there was a knock at the front door. She opened it to find herself confronted by a man in a long, ginger-coloured coat and a deerstalker hat. His gloved hands rested before him on a silver-knobbed cane, and his face was ornamented by a flamboyant moustache with waxed, upturned tips as sharp as stag-horns.

35

'Good evening, my dear,' he said. 'Is your father at home?'

Lucy hesitated. Most of the people who came to the door now were demanding money owed to them, and she was in the habit of saying Mr Bellman was out.

'I think he'll want to see me,' the man went on smoothly. 'Winterthorn is the name—Xavier Winterthorn.' His eyes were almost the same colour as his coat, a light, yellowish brown.

Glancing uneasily behind her, Lucy was glad to see her father coming down the stairs. He advanced with unusual willingness. 'Come in, Mr Winterthorn, come in. This is a great pleasure!'

Lucy closed the door as the two men shook hands in the narrow hall, then waited, unable to get past them to go back into the shop.

'This is my daughter, Lucy,' Jeremy said. 'You'll hardly remember her.'

'Oh, come, come,' said the man in the ginger coat. 'I may not have set foot in the house for some years, but I have observed you and your family from afar. I am familiar with your charming daughter.' He raised Lucy's hand to his lips and gave it a bristly kiss, then returned his attention to her father. 'We need a little talk, I feel.'

'Of course, of course.' Lucy's father seemed flustered. 'What can I offer you? We may be temporarily out of sherry—'

'I never drink,' said Winterthorn, 'as you should remember, Jeremy. A cup of tea, perhaps?' He was moving towards the stairs as if he knew his way to the first-floor sitting room.

'Lucy, could you—'

'Yes, Papa.'

Lucy made her way to the kitchen. Her father's strained joviality had given way to anxiety as he looked at her, and she wondered uneasily who the man could be. Nobody answered when she tapped at the kitchen door, so she went in.

A strong smell of onion soup came from a big pot on the stove, but Ada was not in the room. The Duke turned his blank-eyed face from where he sat at the table with his boy beside him and asked, 'Who's that?'

'Her that lives here,' said the boy.

'I need some tea for my father's visitor,' Lucy said firmly.

'Tea!' The blind man gave a bark of laughter. 'Take him a pint of ale, girl. There's plenty in the jug, no one but me drinking it. George here don't drink, do you, boy?'

George cast an envious look at the jug and said, 'I wouldn't mind.'

The Duke aimed a cuff at him and connected surprisingly well, clouting the boy across the top of the head.

'Our visitor doesn't drink, either,' said Lucy, feeling sorry for George.

'Doesn't he, now?' The Duke angled his head thoughtfully to one side, though the pale blue glass eye still gazed at nothing. 'Well, well. I wonder who that could be?'

Lucy didn't answer. She moved the iron kettle to stand on the hottest part of the stove beside the soup pot, and went to look for cups. All of them were dirty, and there was no water in the ewer that stood by the sink. She took it outside and filled it from the pump in the yard, washed two cups and saucers, then looked for a tray. The wooden one with the carved handles was not there any more, so she had to settle for a rather bent tin one. She washed a small jug and put some milk in it from the dubious-smelling churn, and found some congealed sugar in a bowl. The knitted tea-cosy was stained and unravelling, but it was the best she could do.

As she passed the table with her tray, the Duke said, 'Open the door for the lady, George—where's your manners?'

The skinny boy got reluctantly to his feet—but the Duke hadn't finished. 'This gentleman upstairs,' he said in Lucy's direction. 'His name wouldn't be Winterthorn, by any chance?'

'Yes.' Lucy was too startled to think of refusing to answer.

'Thought as much,' said the blind man. 'Xavier Winterthorn, well, well. Mr X, your friend and mine.' Lucy realized he was slightly drunk. 'Never touches a drop, does Xavier. Never did. Tell him Marmaduke Evans sends his regards, girl.' He fished with a bulky thumb and forefinger in the top pocket of his waistcoat, brought out nothing at all and offered it to Lucy with a courtly gesture. 'My card,' he said.

'Yes. Thank you.' Unnerved, Lucy took the invisible card from him and went out. The boy shut the door behind her. As she made her way along the passage, she could hear the Duke laughing.

When she'd delivered the tea to the sitting room, Lucy went down to the shop, where Tom and Finn were busy folding the piles of clothes left in chaos by the day's rummaging and buying. Tom glanced at her face, then said to his small brother, 'That'll do, Finn. You nip along to the kitchen. I'll come and make supper for us both in a minute.'

He looked guarded when Lucy asked him about the man in the ginger coat. 'I've heard them talk about him,' he admitted.

'Heard who?'

'The kitchen people.'

'What did they say? What does Mr Winterthorn want with Papa?'

38

'I don't know,' said Tom, putting a coat back on the rack. He was avoiding her eye. He turned to pick up another jacket, but Lucy put her hand over his, stopping him.

'You do know,' she said.

Tom pulled away. 'It's only gossip. It could be all wrong, and it's nothing to do with me, anyway.'

Lucy lost her temper. '*Tom!* Can't you see, I want to help Papa. I'm not some silly china doll that's got to be kept safe. If the gossip's wrong, it's not your fault, but I need to know what they're saying. So *tell* me!'

It was the closest they had ever come to a real argument. For a moment they glared at each other, then Tom shrugged. 'Well, all right, only don't blame me if it's rubbish. Ada says this house rightfully belongs to Mr X, as they call him. Don't ask me why,' he rushed on. 'I've never understood. But they all seem to think it's true. The Duke says the house will be his one day, not Winterthorn's—but he's off his head, so you don't want to take any notice of that.' Tom went on working as he spoke, putting clothes on hangers, folding blouses and shirts and underwear.

Lucy watched him, frowning. She struggled to take in this latest piece of bizarre news, then gave up. She would have to ask Papa—if she dared. Ever since his cold anger when she had mentioned his gambling, she had known she must be careful. There were things he would not talk about, and she loved him too much to upset him. 'I'll help you,' she said to Tom. Her mind was still in a turmoil as she shook out skirts and petticoats and laid them in their places on the stacked tables, but it was better to be doing something than nothing.

'Thanks,' said Tom.

There were more people in the kitchen when Lucy went

in with Tom. Ada had come back, and the man called Slip was sitting at the table with the Duke and his boy, all of them eating soup with hunks of bread. A couple of women were chatting beside the stove. Finn was sitting by himself on a bench by the wall.

'Didn't you get any soup?' asked Tom, and the little boy shook his head.

'I've only got one pair of hands,' snapped Ada. Then she saw Lucy and added, 'What are you doing here? You'll get yours later, with your pa.'

'If Mr X says he can,' put in Slip, and he and the Duke both laughed.

'Why shouldn't Lucy come in the kitchen?' Tom asked bravely. 'She lives here.'

'None of your lip,' said Ada. 'And as to living here— well, we'll see, won't we.'

Lucy stared at her, and felt her temper rise. 'What do you mean?' she asked.

Ada turned away without answering. The women glanced at each other and giggled, and Slip whistled a snatch of tune, eyebrows raised above his blue-scarred nose. The Duke wiped his mouth on the back of his hand and pushed his soup bowl across the table. 'I'll have some more of that,' he said.

Ada took his bowl to the stove and refilled it. Then she said to Lucy, 'You just get upstairs, young miss, and mind your own business.'

Tears of fury stung Lucy's eyes, but she was not brave enough to stay in the kitchen, even though Tom took her hand and squeezed it. Keeping her head high, she went out of the door, then ran up the stairs to her room.

She sat on her bed, breathless with anger, for what seemed a long time, waiting for sounds of her father's visitor leaving. At last she heard their footsteps going down to the front door, but she still did not move.

40

Her father tapped at her door. 'Lucy, are you coming down to dinner?'

For a moment, she made no answer. Dinner would be Ada's onion soup, and she wanted nothing to do with it. But she couldn't blame Papa. She went out to join him.

Neither of them spoke as they ate the soup and bread in the cold dining room, drank the cup of tea which followed and then retreated up the stairs. Lucy's father put a couple of small lumps of coal on the fire and dusted his hands fastidiously, sitting back in his chair. There was very little furniture left in the room now. He cleared his throat and said, 'My dear, I have something to tell you.'

'Yes, Papa.' She dreaded what he was going to say, but nothing could be worse than not knowing.

'It's quite a long story,' said Jeremy. 'It goes back to when you were born, sweetheart. As you know, your mother died.'

'Yes,' Lucy said again.

Her father leaned forward a little, hands clasped on his knees. 'A good wife in the house is very valuable, Lucy. Not just for her loving presence, but for the work she does. Seeing that the house runs properly, caring for her family, planning the meals, managing the household staff and budget. Without her, a man can only turn to paid help.'

Lucy nodded. There had been a nanny, and various maids. There was still Ada.

'It cost a bit,' Jeremy went on. 'I had inherited this house from my father, together with the shop—it was a higher-class business in those days—but I was always a little short of what I needed. Keeping up a supply of stock was difficult.'

Silence fell again. 'So what did you do, Papa?' Lucy prompted.

Her father sighed. 'Mr Winterthorn, whom you met this

41

evening, is a rich man. He owned several houses in this street. I knew he would lend money against the security of a house—he had done it for several people. So I approached him.'

'What does "security" mean, Papa?'

'You know, perhaps, that a pawnbroker will lend money against the value of an article—a watch, say, or a piece of jewellery?'

Or a silver pin-cushion. 'Yes.'

'Well, a house can be used in the same way,' her father went on. 'It's called a mortgage. People often borrow money through a mortgage in order to buy a house in the first place—but it doesn't truly belong to them until the loan is paid off.'

So that was it. 'And if the debt is not paid off,' Lucy managed to say, 'then the house belongs to the man who lent the money.'

'Yes.' Jeremy's voice was husky. 'And that's what has happened to me, my darling. I've run out of time.'

Lucy knelt at his feet as she used to when she was small, and took his hands in hers. 'You couldn't help it,' she said.

The single lamp in the room was turned low, casting deep shadows over her father's face. He stroked the back of her hands with his thumbs. 'I've seen men win such riches,' he said, and his eyes looked beyond her, into some dream. 'One must not lose courage.' Then his gaze shifted to meet hers. 'The day is coming, pet lamb,' he told her. 'Quite soon, it will be my turn for the fortune.'

His glittering stare in the shadowed dimness was unblinking, and Lucy felt a chill run through her. *He has a madness,* she thought. *Almost like the dreadful man downstairs. Only Papa could never be dreadful.* Aloud, she said unsteadily, 'What is to happen now? If the house belongs to Mr Winterthorn, will we have to leave?'

'No. He is a generous man, he says we can stay. But there will be changes.' Jeremy released Lucy's hands and sat back. 'We can have a small room upstairs, at a cheap rent.'

'But this won't be our sitting room?'

'No.'

A painful tightness was building up in Lucy's throat, but she did her best to ignore it. 'At least there's the shop,' she said.

A new silence grew. 'Papa?'

'The business will not be mine any more. For the purposes of the mortgage, the shop is part of the house. I made him promise that Tom and Finn can stay on, though,' her father added with a flicker of pride.

The last question had to be asked. 'But, Papa—how will we live?'

'I can give flute lessons. Not here, of course, but I dare say I can go to people's houses. I'll put up a card. Several cards.'

The broken fragments of her life were whirling in Lucy's mind, and one of them jabbed at her painfully. 'I'll have to stop going to school.'

Her father gave a defensive shrug, then said, 'You're a clever girl, my darling. You don't need to be taught. Clever people can educate themselves.'

Lucy struggled to find something reassuring to say, and failed. The sob which had been mounting could not be held off any longer, and in shame as well as anguish, she got up and ran from the room.

5

The next morning was a Saturday, and it was raining hard. Lucy came down to the dining room to find no sign of any breakfast things, and wondered for a moment if Ada had forgotten to set the table. Then she realized that everything had changed. The house didn't belong to Papa any more—it was Mr Winterthorn's. Ada would know all about that. She'd probably known for weeks. The kitchen people seemed to know everything.

Lucy wondered what to do. There was nobody in the kitchen except Slip, who sat at the table eating a cold sausage and stirring a mug of tea, so she went to look in the shop.

Ada was there, talking to Tom. 'None of the stuff on this table is to go for less than ninepence,' she was saying. 'And it's all to be priced. I've written the labels, and there's pins in the box.'

Tom said, 'Does Mr Bellman want—'

'Never mind Mr Bellman,' Ada snapped. 'I'm in charge now. So don't argue, just get on with it.'

Finn, standing beside his brother, gave Lucy an anxious look and seemed about to come over to her, but she put her finger on her lips to deter him, then backed quietly out of the door and retreated along the passage. The blue-scarred man called Slip was still in the kitchen, but she ignored him. Whatever else was going on, Papa would need some breakfast. She collected two plates and two knives and put them on the tin tray. There was half a loaf

44

in the bread-bin. She cut four slices off it, spooned some tea into the pot and poured in water from the steaming kettle.

Slip swallowed some of his own tea, and eyed the bread on Lucy's tray. 'Did Ada say you could have that?' he asked.

'I don't have to ask Ada,' Lucy said with a flare of anger.

The man grinned. 'I reckon you do,' he said. 'She's in charge now. Mr X said.'

'When did he say?' Winterthorn had gone straight out last night, without looking in at the kitchen. Lucy had heard her father show him to the door.

'A good time ago,' Slip said. 'We been waiting for the day to come, that's all.'

Lucy heard her father go into the dining room, so she picked up the tray and went to join him.

They had hardly finished their meagre breakfast when they heard a knock at the front door, followed by Ada's voice and Winterthorn's, loud in the hall and coming closer. Jeremy got to his feet hastily, wiping his mouth with his napkin, as the two entered the room without knocking.

'You have a gentleman's instincts, Jeremy,' Winterthorn said jovially. 'Rising late, enjoying a leisured breakfast. Very nice. Don't let me disturb you. Ada can show me round.'

Lucy's father drew himself up. 'No, I'll come myself— we'd just finished.'

'Excellent,' said Winterthorn. 'We'll make a start, then.' He produced a notebook and pencil from an inside pocket of the ginger coat. 'Nothing down here but the kitchen and this room, right? The shop takes up the rest of the ground floor.' He glanced round the cold dining room and made a note. 'This will do for Daisy. Get a double bed in, Ada, wash-stand and a couple of chairs. All this stuff can go.'

Jeremy frowned in perplexity. 'But where are people to eat?' he asked.

'In the kitchen,' said Winterthorn. He led the way along the passage and up the stairs. In the sitting room, he nodded with satisfaction. 'Plenty of space here—it'll take six beds easily, maybe more. Get rid of the chairs and the bookcase, of course. And there's a small bedroom at the back, I believe.' He walked across the landing to Jeremy's room and flung open the door. 'Ada, I want you and the Duke in here. Handy to see who's going in and out. Keep an eye on things.'

'Yes, sir,' said Ada, with her dreadful smile.

Lucy stared at the floor, feeling hot colour flood her face. Ada and the Duke, living as man and wife in Papa's bedroom? The idea was too embarrassing to contemplate.

On the next floor, Winterthorn tried the door of the front room occupied by Albert Apps, and found it locked. He produced a bunch of keys from his pocket and opened it. Albert wasn't there, of course—he always left early in order to be at his work in a lawyer's office by half past eight. The room was very neat, the bed made and no possessions lying about. Two books and a few letters and papers were tidily arranged on the small table by the window, but that was all.

'Just one tenant,' Ada said, gesturing at the big room. 'Terrible waste.'

'Soon get rid of him,' said Winterthorn.

'That's impossible!' Jeremy was outraged. 'Albert Apps has a legal contract for a year's tenancy.'

'When was it renewed?' Winterthorn enquired.

'On the Michaelmas Quarter Day—only three weeks ago.'

'I see.' Unruffled, Winterthorn made another note, then

turned and led the way to Lucy's room, where he opened the door and walked in. It looked pink and cosy, and Lucy felt proud of it. She had tidied the bed as she did each morning, and her rag doll, Mary Jane, was propped against the pillows in her usual place, taking care of things.

'As before, Ada,' Winterthorn said over his shoulder. 'Clear all this stuff and get beds in. Three or four, I'd think.'

'But where am I to put everything?' Lucy asked in anguish, and at the same time, her father burst out, 'You're turning the place into a common lodging house!'

'Correct,' agreed Winterthorn, ignoring Lucy. 'As you should have done years ago, Jeremy, had you had an ounce of business sense.'

Jeremy put his hands over his face, and Winterthorn walked past him, starting up the narrow stairs that led to the top floor.

'Just the two small rooms up here,' Ada said, as if she owned them. 'I've been in this one all these years, young Tom and his brother next door. Tom's not a bad worker,' she added, 'but you want to get rid of the little 'un. Never make anything of him, all bent up like that. Useless.'

'I could have a use for him,' said Winterthorn. 'We'll see. The boys can stay there for the time being, anyway.' Then he turned to Lucy's father. 'You and your daughter, Jeremy, can have the other room up here—the one that's been Ada's. A little small, perhaps, but I won't charge you much.'

Jeremy glanced into the poky attic room with its sloping ceiling, then his eyes slid away. 'Thank you,' he whispered. His face was ashen.

When Winterthorn had gone, Ada's friends came out of

the kitchen like a swarm of ants, invading all the rooms to lay hold of the remaining furniture and bundle it down the stairs. A man with a donkey cart loaded up armchairs, fire-irons, bookshelves, curtains, the hearthrug from the sitting room, Papa's writing desk—all the things Lucy had known from her earliest childhood. Her bed was carried up to the attic room and pushed in beside her father's, the two separated by only a foot or two of space. The place was otherwise bare except for a crate which served as a table, a couple of shelves, and a few hooks on which to hang clothes.

The house began to sound different as it emptied. Its old, cosy murmur changed to an echoing hollowness, and all its comfortable familiarity was gone.

'Why have they taken the stair carpets up?' Jeremy asked in bewilderment, and Ada, overhearing, said, 'They get mucky with people in and out. Saves cleaning.'

Jeremy retreated to the attic room and sat silently on his bed, holding the flute in its case on his lap. He did not answer when Lucy spoke to him, and his eyes stared at nothing. In these few hours, he seemed to have become an old man.

Lucy gave up trying to comfort him. It was more important now to retrieve what she could of the things that had belonged to them. She took her father's clothes from the chest of drawers which still stood in his room and gathered up his slippers and nightshirt, his dressing gown, and his few remaining books, carrying them in armfuls up to the room where he sat in silence.

In her own room, two men with a ladder were taking down her curtains.

'Oh, please!' Lucy said. 'Can't I have them?'

'Orders,' said the man. 'Everything's to go. You'll get paid for what was yours.'

Lucy picked up Mary Jane from where she lay on the

bare boards of the floor and held her familiar cloth body tightly, then found Finn beside her. 'I came to help,' he said. 'Tom sent me.'

'Oh, Finn, thank you.'

The patchwork quilt from Lucy's bed was lying on the bare boards of the floor, and while the men weren't looking she bundled it into the little boy's arms then added Mary Jane. 'Can you manage all that?'

'Yes,' he said, and limped determinedly away.

The men rolled up the curtains, together with Lucy's bedside rug. While they were gone, she grabbed up some clothes and a couple of books and carried them upstairs. Then, meeting the men on their way back from the street, she ran down and approached the driver of the donkey cart, who sat on one of the shafts, smoking a clay pipe.

'The curtains,' she said breathlessly, 'there's been a mistake, they're wanted.'

The donkey man took his pipe from his mouth and said, 'Nothing to do with me. When the cart's full I drives it, that's all.' And put his pipe back again.

Lucy hauled the curtains off and rolled them in a fringed shawl that her father had always kept because it had belonged to Lucy's mother. She took the rug as well, and lugged her load upstairs. She hid in the sitting room while the men came past with her wardrobe, then went on up to the attic. Her father was still sitting on his bed.

'Papa,' Lucy said gently, 'do you think you could find a piece of string?' Perhaps it would be good for him to move about, doing some little task rather than sitting in misery.

He looked at her as if he didn't know what the word meant. 'String,' he repeated.

'Yes. If we had some string, we could hang these curtains between our beds, then it would be more like having a room each.'

After a few moments, her father said, 'I suppose so.' His face was still very white, and when he got to his feet, he swayed as if he might fall.

'It's all right,' Lucy said, alarmed. 'I'll go.'

He stood irresolutely, still clutching the flute. 'Could you? I don't feel quite—'

'Sit down, Papa. Can I get you anything? Some water?'

'No, thank you.' He sat down again, then lay down and turned on his side as if he was cold.

Lucy covered him with her quilt, and was glad to see Finn coming in with another load. 'Stay here with my father,' she said. 'If he needs anything, will you come and tell me?'

'Yes,' the little boy said gravely.

'Thank you.' She herself was filled with an impatient energy, and she was glad of it. As long as she kept moving, she could fend off the misery which had engulfed her father.

By the evening, Lucy ached all over from running up and down stairs and carrying things. The room that had been hers now had four narrow iron beds crammed into it with barely a space between them. She stood and looked at it for a moment, then turned away. Compared with such bareness, the attic room she shared with her father was almost cosy, stuffed as it was with whatever possessions she had been able to retrieve.

On the first-floor landing she nearly collided with Albert Apps at the door of his room. He raised his hat to her with his usual courtesy, but his face with the drooping moustache was shocked. 'Whatever has happened?' he asked.

Lucy found it hard to meet his eye. 'The house doesn't belong to Papa any more.'

'Then who has it? And why has my door been unlocked?'

'Mr Winterthorn. He's got a key.'

'Winterthorn!' Albert looked startled. 'Is he involved in this?' He ran his fingers through his thinning hair. 'I didn't know your father was in quite such trouble. Do please give him my condolences, Lucy.'

'Yes, I will.' Papa had been right, Lucy thought, as she watched Albert go into his room. Mr Apps was a good person to have in the house. His little complaints about the flute seemed trivial now compared with the ruination that had happened. 'Thank you,' she added. And Albert gave her a brief smile before closing the door.

When she went back upstairs, her father was awake, staring round him as if recovering from a dream. He swung his legs to the floor. 'Lucy, where is my coat?' he asked.

'Here, look.' She had hung it on a nail behind the door. Jeremy was getting to his feet. 'Papa, are you going out?'

'I need some air.' He was putting his coat on, and there was a new determination in his face. 'I'll bring us both something to eat—don't go down to that kitchen.'

'No, Papa,' Lucy promised, a little reluctantly.

Her father picked up his flute and went out.

At least he's better, Lucy thought. But she wished he hadn't forbidden her to go downstairs. A good smell of frying onions was coming from the kitchen, and she was ravenously hungry. Ada's friends didn't frighten her as much as they frightened her father. He'd never had anything to do with such people except as customers coming to the shop, and that was different. He was a kind man, always inclined to let garments go for less than their value, but there was no mixing of the buyers' world and his. They'd never been real to him as they now were to Lucy.

51

She stared round the small, cluttered room. Ada had lived here for—how many years? Four or five, probably. While Lucy and her father had the whole house except for Albert's room, their servant was up here, living a life neither of them thought about. They'd never known what she did when she wasn't lighting fires or cleaning or cooking, whether she had friends or what she said to them. *Well, you know now*, Lucy said to herself. And secretly, she felt slightly proud of that knowledge, because mixing with the kitchen people made her feel grown-up and tough, even though they scared her. She almost wanted to know more, finding it weirdly fascinating that they cared so little for manners and fine possessions—all the things she'd been brought up to think important. Meanwhile, she was hungry and bored, and it would be a long time before her father came back. She got up and tapped on Tom's door, then looked in to see if he was there.

The room was empty but for a few discarded clothes and a clutter of wood shavings on the small table by the window together with a half-finished toy boat—Tom was always whittling at something. But now, he and Finn would be down in the forbidden kitchen, eating whatever it was that went with the fried onions. Lucy went back and sat on her bed. Her books lay on the floor—*Gulliver's Travels*, *Pilgrim's Progress*, *Songs for the Nursery*, *The Blind Child*, *Peep of Day*—but she felt too lonely and hungry to read. She reached for Mary Jane and sat hugging her for company.

Time passed. At last a footstep sounded on the uncarpeted stairs, and Lucy put the doll down quickly. She got to her feet, brushing her skirt to try and make herself a bit smarter. Papa must not find her looking miserable.

Someone knocked at the door. Not Papa, then—he would have come straight in.

'Who is it?' Lucy called.

'Winterthorn. Is your father there?'

Lucy opened the door. 'He had to go out. Can I take a message?'

'Give him this.' Winterthorn thrust an envelope into her hand. 'Tell him it's for the furniture.'

'Yes,' said Lucy.

There was a pause. The man's light brown eyes looked her over, then met her gaze with a disturbing directness. 'You'll be needing an income, the pair of you.'

Lucy waited. She had been thinking about this very thing for the last hour. How were they to live without the shop? Her father's hopes of giving flute lessons had not sounded very convincing.

'You could earn a bit,' Winterthorn said. 'You're small for your age, but you look strong enough. Ada will need help—this is a big place for her to run on her own, boarders in and out all the time. If you want a job as her assistant, I'll pay you half a crown a week. Cash in your hand, mind, it won't go to your pa. That'll cover the rent if he hasn't got it.'

Lucy felt her face flush with embarrassment. So this man knew about Papa's gambling. He knew, too, that he was unlikely to get his rent money unless Lucy earned it. But would there be anything left over? They would need money for food, as well.

'How much is the rent?' she asked.

'Two bob.' His foxy eyes glinted with amusement. 'You catch on quick, don't you?'

'So I'd have sixpence left.' She and Papa couldn't live on sixpence. 'It isn't enough.'

'It will be if his lordship earns a bob or two,' said Winterthorn. 'I'm doing you a favour—take it or leave it.'

There was no choice.

'I'll take it,' said Lucy. 'When do I start?'

'Tomorrow morning, half past five. Goodnight to you.'
He turned and went down the stairs.

Never be afraid of work, her grandmother had said. Lucy sat down on her bed with the envelope in her hands. There were several coins in it, and she wondered how much Winterthorn had paid them for the furniture. Maybe there was a folded five-pound note as well, in which case they would be all right for quite a long time, and she need not rush into becoming Ada's servant. She looked down at the pencilled scrawl on the front.

Bellman 5*s*. 6*d*.

Five shillings and sixpence. It was a ridiculously small amount for all the things that had been loaded onto the donkey cart and driven away. Enough to pay two weeks' rent on this attic room, but not three.

An awful thought was growing in Lucy's mind. If she gave this money to Papa, it would all be gone in one night of wild hope.

Keep it.

The words sounded clear in her head, as if someone else had spoken them—her grandmother, perhaps, or even her lost mother. Lucy bent down and hauled out her treasure box, which she had retrieved from her room before anything else and put for safe keeping under her bed. She pushed the envelope of coins into it, underneath the special things she kept there—a brooch, a shell, some ribbons, a bundle of letters from her grandmother, a bag of beautifully coloured glass marbles, a canary's feather. Then she closed the lid and guiltily returned the box to its hiding place. This deceit of Papa was the most awful thing she had ever done.

For the next long half-hour, Lucy wondered if she should get the money out again and put it on her father's bed for him to find when he returned—but she knew she could not. Things were too desperate for that. Only the other day, a man had shouted at Papa in the street, 'You should be in Newgate!'

Everyone knew about Newgate, the terrible prison where people were locked up with iron fetters on their legs. Sometimes a man or woman would be hanged there, and half London flocked to watch. The debtors' prison at Southwark was even closer to home, only a few streets away, and behind those grey walls were people who had done nothing worse than owe money. As her papa did. Lucy sat on her bed with her hands pressed tightly in her lap, sick with anxiety and determination. If five shillings and sixpence could keep them safe for a week or two longer, then she must guard it carefully and use it only for real needs. But she wished with all her heart that she had not been put in charge of it.

Her father looked triumphant when he came in. He was clutching his flute, together with a loaf of bread and a greasy parcel which gave off a wonderful smell. 'Fried fish!' he said. 'I was lucky, my darling. You see, it can happen!' He sat down beside her. 'Do we have a knife to cut the bread?'

Lucy shook her head, too hungry to answer. She tore a hunk off the loaf and bit into it, then took a piece of the succulent, still-warm fish. Jeremy went on between mouthfuls. 'I made a little money playing my flute. Not a lot, but enough to put into a game of Three-up. And I won! I could have won more,' he added with regret, 'only the others had lost all they had, and wouldn't pledge their jackets or scarves. So I bought the fish and came home. But my luck has changed, pet lamb, I know it has!' He was eating untidily in his excitement, dropping flakes of fish, all the shock of the day forgotten.

He wants me to be pleased, Lucy thought. Secretly, she

found her father a little alarming when he spoke with such passion of the fortune that luck would bring him one day. She could not believe in it, and this new lack of faith in her beloved papa's judgement made her feel lonely and secretive. But it was no use pretending. She was like the people in the market when the preachers came with their tambourines and banners, assuring them of God's love. The stallholders and traders stood with bowed heads and looked suitably humble, because the preachers often handed out free oranges when the prayers were over. They took the fruit, but Lucy had seen their shrugs and grins as soon as the black-coated figures moved on. She used to be shocked by such cynicism, but she saw it differently now. Why should the market people believe that Heaven would look kindly on them? Their lives had always been hard, and they were likely to remain so.

Licking the grease off her fingers, Lucy wondered if luck was God's way of organizing things, and if so, why some people had so little when others had so much. *Perhaps you have to ask*, she thought. *Tonight, I must remember to say my prayers.* It was a habit that had begun to slip away with her childhood, and she was not absolutely sure that God was listening. But as things were now, she needed any help she could get.

6

In what seemed like the middle of the night, Ada banged on the door of Lucy's room and shouted, 'Out of that bed!'

Lucy heard her father move sharply on his side of the curtain, but, to her relief, his gentle snores began again almost at once. She had not managed to tell him about helping Ada, and neither had she mentioned Winterthorn's visit last night. If her father had asked about payment for the furniture, she could not have lied to him—and yet a deception had arisen through her silence. She dressed quietly and slipped out of the room.

She went to the privy in the yard then washed her hands and face under the pump, but Ada saw her from the scullery window and shouted, 'Never mind about that—get in here and see to this stove.'

Lucy had no idea how to light a stove. Impatiently instructed by Ada, she raked out the still-hot ash, leaving the embers, then added sticks of thin kindling and crouched by the fire-bars with the leather bellows, blowing the fire into life.

'Lucky it's still in,' said Ada. 'Most mornings, it's not.'

Lucy didn't answer. The hot sparks prickled in her throat and made her nose run, and having no handkerchief, she rubbed her nose on the back of her dirty hand. It was the first time she had ever done such a thing. She got to her feet and took the bucket of ash out to empty it in the yard.

'Fill it with coal while you're out there,' Ada shouted after her. 'You should have brought the coal in before you lit the stove.'

'Yes,' said Lucy. 'Sorry.'

'Got no sense,' muttered Ada.

It was true, Lucy thought as she washed her hands again in the cold yard after filling the bucket. When it came to this sort of thing, she had no sense at all, because it was so strange to her.

When the stove was safely alight, water had to be fetched from the pump and set to boil, and then Ada sent Lucy down to the baker's to get three loaves. After that she was grudgingly allowed a cup of tea and a hunk of bread, then she had to clean the hall and stairs.

A couple of hours later, Lucy was scrubbing the front doorstep when her father came out with his coat on. He stared at her, astounded. 'Lucy, what are you doing?'

'Helping Ada.' She rinsed her brush in the bucket, surprised to find herself impatient with his dismay.

'But—'

Lucy moved aside to let him pass, as any servant girl would. 'It's only for a while,' she said. 'Until things get better.'

'I was looking for you. I was going to take you with me to see Miss Martin.' Jeremy didn't seem to have understood what she had said. 'Since it's a Sunday and the girls won't be there—I thought it was the best day. There might be things you want to bring home. Books, perhaps . . . ' His voice tailed off.

'No,' said Lucy, stony-faced. 'No, there's nothing.' She turned away and rubbed the block of soap across the wet bristles of the brush. *Nothing, nothing.* She was glad this work prevented her from going to the school. It would have been so painful to see Miss Martin one last time, only to say goodbye. She turned to her scrubbing again.

Her father watched her for a few moments more, then he walked away along the street.

By the evening, Lucy was still working, this time filling mugs with ale from a barrel that had been brought into the kitchen and stood on trestles by the wall. The day had been a hard one and her stomach ached with hunger. The spicy smell of saveloy sausages boiling in a pot on the stove made her mouth water, and most of the other people in the room were already eating.

Ada was hacking up bread at the table. 'Saveloys a halfpenny,' she bawled as two more men came into the crowded room. 'With mustard and a slice.'

'Can I have one?' Lucy asked. 'Please?'

Ada glared at her. 'Where's your money?'

'I haven't got any,' Lucy said, too ravenous to be scared. 'You can take it out of my wages at the end of the week.'

'It's not me as pays you,' Ada said. But she fished a red-skinned sausage out of the bubbling water, dipped it in the mustard pot and laid it in a folded hunk of bread, then handed it over.

'Thank you.' Lucy didn't like mustard, but she wasn't going to argue. She looked round for somewhere to sit down, and a girl with yellow-dyed hair moved along to make a space on the bench.

'Take the weight off your feet, love,' she said, 'you look all in. What's your name?'

'Lucy.' The bread and hot sausage tasted wonderful.

'I'm called Daisy. D'you work here?'

Lucy nodded, because her mouth was too full to say anything.

The man called Slip leaned across and said, 'Her pa used to own the place.' He grinned at Lucy. 'Bit of a come-down, eh?'

'You leave her alone,' said Daisy. 'She's all right, aren't you, dear?'

'Yes,' said Lucy.

The blue-scarred man shrugged and went to join his friends who stood round the beer barrel. Ada was serving them herself now.

'How old are you?' Daisy asked. 'Eleven, twelve?'

'Nearly thirteen.' It was Lucy's birthday very soon, but she knew there was nothing to look forward to this year. No presents, no girls invited home for tea—not that she minded about that. She'd always hated the way they glanced at the door to the shop and stifled giggles behind their hands.

'Lovely,' said Daisy. 'I wish I was thirteen again.'

'Do you?' Lucy was surprised. It was usually old people who said that kind of thing, regretting their lost youth, but Daisy seemed young herself, not more than fifteen or sixteen.

'I'd have done things different,' Daisy said. 'But I didn't know, did I? You can't choose one way or the other if you don't know what you're getting into; it just happens. That's your luck, I suppose.'

'Papa says luck can change,' Lucy said, but Daisy shook her head.

'I reckon you just got to make the best of it,' she said. 'Some are born lucky, some aren't.' She got up and brushed a few crumbs off her blouse. 'Better get out and do some work, I suppose, before the Duke starts complaining.' She stooped to pick up her shawl from where it lay on the bench, and said in Lucy's ear, 'Be careful, sweetheart. Don't do anything you'll regret.' Then she went to the back door and let herself out into the night.

When Lucy had finished eating, she slipped out of the kitchen before Ada noticed her, and went to find Tom.

Although it was nearly eight o'clock, he was still attending to customers in the shop.

'I thought you closed at six,' Lucy said.

'Not now.' Tom dropped some coins into the till and closed the drawer. 'They want the place open longer hours.'

Lucy knew who he meant. 'Ada and the Duke.'

Tom nodded as he pushed a coat back into its place on the rail. He glanced round to make sure he was not overheard, then said, 'And that's not all.'

'What do you mean?'

Tom took a breath to answer, but a woman with a sleeping child held in one arm came up and asked, 'Take twopence halfpenny for this blouse, love? It's marked threepence, but it's torn under the arm.'

'Sorry,' Tom told her. 'I'm not allowed to reduce the prices.'

The woman gave him a disgusted look. 'Mr Bellman was never like that,' she said. 'Always reasonable, he was.'

An older woman came up behind her to join in the argument, and Tom made a despairing face at Lucy. No hope of talking just now.

'I'll see you later,' she said.

Her father was not in the small room, but a book lay on Lucy's bed. She picked it up, and found it was the Latin primer she had used at school. Inside its cover was a folded sheet of paper.

Dear Lucy,

It is God's will to send us mixed fortune, perhaps to enable us to find a strength we were unaware of. Try to keep up your studies; it will help you to respect yourself when times seem hard.

Your father is waiting, so I must be brief. I will be happy to hear from you at any time, please remember that.

With affectionate wishes,

Emmeline Martin.

Lucy sat down with the letter in her hand. She read the lines of graceful writing again, and tears pricked her eyes at the knowledge of what she had lost.

There was a light tap at the door, and she opened it to find little Finn standing there.

'Tom sent me,' he said. He sounded important.

'That's nice.' Lucy smiled at him and gave her eyes a quick rub. 'Come in. Sit yourself down.'

Finn sat on the bed, his twisted leg dangling its usual few inches short of the other foot. 'Tom said I was to tell you about my job—he was going to tell you in the shop, only he was too busy.'

'Yes, he was.' A faint warning sounded in Lucy's mind. Tom had sent the little boy as a messenger, and Finn might not understand the full truth of what he was going to say. 'So what's this job, Finn? Who are you going to work for?'

'Mr Marmaduke,' Finn said proudly. 'I'm going to help him.'

'You mean the man who can't see? The one they call the Duke?'

'Yes. And the others, too. The blue-nose man, and there's one with ginger hair, and a big one with tattoos on his arms. It'll be at night.' The little boy was round-eyed with excitement and new responsibility. 'And I'm not to tell anyone cos it's a secret.'

'Goodness,' said Lucy. She smiled at him again although her mind was racing through dreadful possibilities. Why would these men take a child with them on some expedition after dark? 'But the Duke's already got a boy to help him,' she said. 'Why does he need you?'

'George is his daytime boy,' Finn said. 'I'm to be his night-time one.'

'I see.' But there was a lot she didn't see. 'You're only seven—you need your sleep, Finn.'

'Seven's quite big,' Finn argued. 'George was only seven when he started work, and he's eleven now.'

Lucy thought about the scrawny boy who guided the Duke. He was quite tall for his age, with a big head and lanky arms, but he had no more energy than an old cab horse. Half the time, he seemed too tired even to bother talking. 'You don't have to be like George,' she said.

Finn looked at her as if she was being silly. 'But I am like him,' he pointed out. 'Only I've got a funny leg and he hasn't.'

The letter from Miss Martin lay on the bed, and its words spoke silently to Lucy . . . . *respect yourself.* 'Oh, Finn,' she said gently, 'you're much better off than George. Nobody has ever cared for him, and you have people who love you.'

'That's nice,' said Finn, and he put his arms round Lucy's neck and kissed her.

'Have you had anything to eat?' Lucy asked him.

'No. Tom's been too busy, and Ada says I'm not to go in the kitchen on my own, cos I get in the way.'

Oh, does she, Lucy thought. She stood up and gave the little boy her hand. 'Come on—you can come down with me.'

Strangely, Ada didn't argue. She forked a saveloy onto a plate, and Finn said quickly, 'No mustard.'

That was how to do it, Lucy thought—don't waste time in wondering whether a protest was polite, just jump in and say what you mean. But Finn wouldn't have been served at all if she hadn't been there to ask for him. She reached for the loaf and cut him a thick slice of bread, then steered him to the table.

George, the Duke's 'daytime boy', as Finn had called him, sat huddled on a bench by the wall. Lucy looked at him and frowned in concern. He was hunched up like a sick bird, his chin tucked into the collar of his threadbare jacket and his bony arms hugging his chest. Everyone else was sweating in the hot kitchen, but as Lucy watched she saw the boy shiver. She went and sat beside him, timidly putting her hand to his face. He didn't seem aware of her touch, but she could feel the heat of his body even though he was shivering regularly.

The Duke sat on the lad's other side, and Lucy reached forward and touched his sleeve to attract his attention. 'George isn't well,' she said. 'He's got a fever.'

'Just a chill,' said the Duke. 'You don't want to take no notice.' His hand caught hers and he turned his one-eyed china stare towards her. 'That Lucy?'

'Yes.' She tried to pull away, but he held her firmly, leaning across the sick boy to run his other hand up to her shoulder. 'Very nice, you are,' he said. 'Just the right size. You'll do as my guide if the boy snuffs it.'

Lucy looked round for help, and was relieved to see Tom appear at the door. He caught her glance and came straight over. 'I think your father wants you,' he said, and gave her the ghost of a wink.

'Thank you.' She pulled her hand free and stood up.

'Who's old Bellman to give orders?' the Duke complained. 'Nothing, that's what he is.' He thumped his chest with his fist. 'I tell you, I'm the one who runs things round here. Mr X better learn that as well. No good him playing the la-di-da landlord; he's not the man I am. Duke by name and Duke by nature, that's me. This house ought to be mine by rights. The rest of them—they're nothing. Nothing at all.'

Lucy didn't stay to hear any more. She fled up the stairs to her room.

As she expected, her father was not there. She sat down on her bed in the cold attic, tucking her hands under her arms for warmth. After a bit, she unlaced her old boots (the promised new ones had never been mentioned again) and lay down, pulling the quilt over her. She was half asleep when there was a tap at the door, but she jumped up to open it.

'Tom!' she whispered. 'Come in. Is Finn in bed?'

'Yes.' Tom was looking worried as he sat down beside her.

'What's this job he was talking about?' Lucy asked. 'He's too young to be going out with those men at night.'

'Didn't you understand? They're criminals, Lucy, the whole gang of them. Burglars. And the best way to get into a house is to take a boy who's small enough to put through a scullery window or a skylight. No noise, no breaking glass—he just unbolts the door for them. George used to do it, but he's getting too big, and he's clumsy. And now he's ill.'

Lucy's hands were over her mouth in horror. 'But Finn wouldn't do anything like that!'

'Yes, he would,' said Tom grimly. 'He doesn't know yet what he's in for—they'll tell him some tale about it being a friend's house or the keys being lost—but Slip told me to make sure he does exactly as he's told, or it'll be the worse for him.'

'What do you mean?'

For a moment, Tom did not answer. Then he said, 'They might kill him.'

The shock of it made Lucy feel as if she couldn't breathe. A long moment passed, then Tom went on, 'I wish I could get him away from here, but we've no money and nowhere to go. He'd be safer back in the Home, but I'm too old for that now—they only take you until you're twelve. And I couldn't leave him on his own.'

65

Lucy was thinking frantically. Her father had rescued the boys from that grim institution in the first place. 'Perhaps Papa could—'

'No!' Tom gripped her arm hard. 'Lucy, you mustn't tell anyone. Slip warned me. If they find out I've talked—' He didn't have to finish.

'All right, I promise.'

'Cross your heart?'

'Cross my heart.' *And hope to die.* But neither of them added the second half of the vow, and it hung unspoken between them.

Lucy did not hear her father come in that night, but he was asleep in his bed when she tiptoed out the next morning to start another day's work. In the kitchen, George sat huddled by the cold stove. He looked very ill and mumbled that his chest hurt, but the Duke took him out all the same.

The rooms of the house were all occupied now by people who wanted a cheap bed for the night, and the worst job of Lucy's day was dealing with the buckets that were used as lavatories. She had to carry these down to the yard, but the outside privy was only emptied by the night-soil men twice a week, and it was already overflowing.

'Chuck it by the wall,' Ada said and, reluctantly, Lucy did as she was told.

The smell seemed to permeate the whole house, and as Lucy worked through the long day she thought with dismay of how the stench was going to build up in weeks to come. From the windows of the bed-filled dormitory that used to be their sitting room she saw her father go out with his flute in its case and waved to him, but he did not look up.

By six o'clock, Lucy was spooning out potatoes to go with the bloaters that gave off their strong, fishy smell from where they simmered on the stove. 'Three spuds each,' Ada instructed her. 'And one slice of bread. Any more and it's extra.'

At last Lucy took her own meal across to the table where there was a space beside Daisy. They both ate in silence, too hungry to talk. Then Daisy wiped her plate with the last of the bread and said, 'Your pa's good at the flute, isn't he.'

'I didn't know you'd heard him,' said Lucy. Her father had often played in other people's houses, sometimes on his own or with a small group for an evening party, but she couldn't imagine that Daisy would be at one of these.

'Got a pitch down the market, hasn't he,' said Daisy. 'Near the hot-chestnut seller.'

'Oh.'

'Didn't you know?'

Lucy shook her head. So her father was playing in the street for money. And last night, in some game, he would have lost whatever he'd made.

'Nothing wrong with playing in the street,' said Daisy, mistaking the cause of Lucy's silence. Then she added, 'I should know. I just wish I played music, that's all.'

Their eyes met, and with a shock of understanding Lucy suddenly knew why it was that Daisy went out in the evenings. *Better do some work*, she'd said, *before the Duke starts complaining*. It was not long since Lucy had talked to Tom about what she'd called 'women who have to be paid', and here she was, sitting beside one of them as if it was the most natural thing in the world. She felt her face blush scarlet.

Daisy was watching her. 'Don't know much, do you?' she said.

'No,' said Lucy, and felt obscurely ashamed. After a

moment, she put her hand out, and Daisy took it in her own rough, warm one, and held it tight.

The next day was Lucy's thirteenth birthday. Ada banged on the door as usual, and Lucy got up and dressed herself. She was just going out when her father emerged from his side of the curtain in his nightshirt. He kissed her and said, 'Happy birthday, my dear. I want you to have this.' He opened his hand to show her a gold locket on a fine chain.

'Oh, Papa!' She had not expected anything on this birthday, let alone a thing so beautiful and so obviously expensive.

'I kept it for you,' said her father, 'all these years. I was going to keep it longer, until you were a grown woman at twenty-one, but the way things are . . . ' His voice tailed off. 'Look inside it.'

With her thumbnail, Lucy clicked open the catch. A tiny, oval painting of a fair-haired woman gazed serenely up at her, and her heart gave a sudden jump. 'Is it—'

'Your mother, yes. It's the only painting I have of her. It was done a few weeks before you were born. She'd have wanted you to have it.' Jeremy tried to smile. 'It'll be safer with you than me.'

Ada shouted from downstairs. 'Lucy! Hurry up!'

'I'll have to go.' Lucy embraced her father. 'Thank you, Papa—I'll keep it for ever.' She fastened the locket round her neck, but tucked it inside her blouse, where casual eyes could not see it.

'Don't work too hard, sweetheart.'

'I won't.' But she knew the promise was an empty one.

'Washday,' Ada announced. 'Get down to the cellar and light the copper.'

The morning that followed was packed with tasks. As well as the usual housework, Lucy had to haul in water from the pump to fill the copper and boil up seemingly endless mountains of clothes, all of which had to be rubbed on a washboard with hard soap, put through the wringer, rinsed and wrung again. Then she pegged them on the lines stretched across the smelly yard, where they flapped wetly in the wind that blew from the river.

When she came in, blowing on her chilled fingers, Ada said grudgingly, 'Letter for you.'

It was in fact a small package, and Lucy ripped it open eagerly, recognizing her grandmother's neat writing. She began to read the letter inside with hungry attention.

My dear Lucy,

I write to send you loving wishes on your thirteenth birthday. You are a young lady now, not a little girl any more. How I wish I could be with you. I could help you to put your hair up for the first time, and we might go shopping for a long skirt. As it is, I can only send you a few small things, with my fondest love. I think of you often, my dear.

The weather is milder here than in London, but I miss—

'You can read that later,' Ada interrupted. 'There's work to be done, if you don't mind.'

'All right.' But Lucy could not resist looking in the package. It held a tortoiseshell comb, a packet of hairpins, and a small, silver-backed mirror which she recognized. She had seen it often on her grandmother's dressing table.

At lunchtime, Tom came into the kitchen from the shop and gave Lucy a carved bird, and Finn presented her with a sugar bun wrapped in a bit of paper. 'We'll share it,' she said, kissing him. The little boy looked dark round the eyes from lack of sleep, and she glanced at Tom in silent enquiry, getting a slight nod in answer. Yes, Finn had been out with Slip and the other men last night.

Halfway through the afternoon, the front doorbell rang. Lucy went to answer it, wiping her hands on her apron. The Duke stood there between two severe-looking women, both of them carrying Bibles.

'We are from the City Mission,' one of them announced. 'Is this Mr Winterthorn's residence?'

'Um . . . yes,' said Lucy. The Duke had never come to the front door before—he always went in and out through the kitchen. And where was George?

'The child who was with this man collapsed in the street,' said one of the women. 'He has been conveyed to the hospital.'

Ada had come up behind Lucy. 'Well, he was all right this morning,' she said. 'Come on in,' she added to the Duke. 'No need to stand there for everyone to gawp at.'

'He cannot possibly have been all right,' the woman argued as Ada helped the Duke into the hall. 'He has pneumonia. Is he your son?'

'That he's not!' Ada sounded indignant. 'I don't have no brats, and glad of it. The Duke and me gave George a home out of the goodness of our hearts, that's all, and this is the thanks we get.'

The other woman put a gloved hand on Ada's sleeve. 'Will you join us in a prayer for the child?' she asked.

Ada looked at her with contempt. 'You pray if you want to,' she said. 'I've got work to do.' And she shut the door.

Alone in her room that evening, Lucy put the precious locket carefully into her treasure box, together with Tom's carved bird and the presents from her grandmother, and checked that Winterthorn's envelope was still there, with

70

its coins inside it. Then she sat down to read the rest of her grandmother's letter.

I miss the garden and the beehives. I hope the new people at the inn will look after the bees properly when the spring comes and they start to fly again. The house here is very nice, with a view across the sea, but leisure does not suit me, and I have too much time with nothing better to do than think of the days that are gone. I sew and embroider, of course, and read to my sister-in-law, whose eyesight is not good, but the garden is nothing more than a sanded yard behind the house, with a few geraniums in pots. I should not grumble. I have a pleasant room, and the cook does not mind if I invade her kitchen sometimes to make a batch of ginger biscuits.

I think of you often, and wish I was not so far away. Please write again when you can; and remember, I am always ready to help you in any way that my circumstances permit.

> *May God bless you.*
> *With loving wishes,*
> > *your affectionate*
> > *Grandmother*

PS—Please give my best regards to your father.

Lucy folded the letter carefully. In her imagination, she went to her father's writing desk, reached for paper and a pen and opened the lid of the silver inkwell—but these things were all gone.

I don't care, she thought. *Tomorrow I will look for a pencil, and some paper. Nobody can stop me from writing.*

It seemed as if she had joined some kind of fight against all things that were unreasonable and unkind. There was nobody else in her army except Tom and little Finn and her poor papa, and perhaps Daisy. But it made her feel braver.

71

7

Lucy borrowed a pencil from the shop the next day, and Tom gave her some of the small bits of paper that were supposed to be pinned to clothes with the prices written on them. That evening, as soon as she could escape upstairs, she wrote to thank her grandmother for the presents. She told her also about the loss of the house and about Mr Winterthorn, and the dreadful changes that had taken place.

Several times, she paused to wonder how much she should say. Papa had borrowed money from her grandparents—there was no doubt of that. And Grandma probably knew more than Lucy did about the crazy belief that lay behind his difficulties. All the same, it seemed disloyal to mention it, like gossiping about him behind his back. So she just wrote, *Papa is very upset, and I pray that nothing worse will happen.*

Perhaps that was enough. *I too wish you were still in Penge,* she added. *Exeter is so far away. Your loving granddaughter, Lucy.*

She had no envelope, and no money for a stamp. She folded the letter and put it in her pocket, then opened the door of her room. At least she could return the pencil to Tom. But her father was coming up the stairs towards her, with his head down and his hands pushed into his coat pockets. She was shocked by how thin and stoop-shouldered he looked—and then she realized what was wrong. He was not carrying his flute in its black case. He glanced up at her, but walked past into the room without speaking

72

and sat down on his bed, still hunched in his coat. She came back to join him.

'Papa, what's wrong?'

'My accursed luck.' His voice was hardly audible.

'Where is your flute?'

He flared into anger. 'Lucy, mind your own business! What I do with my own possessions is not your affair.'

A few weeks ago, such a retort would have crushed her, but she was used to being shouted at by Ada now, and she felt braver. Besides, this was too important to be left unquestioned. 'Have you sold it?'

'No! I'd never do that. It's just . . . lent for a while.'

A vision of the crowded window under the sign of the three brass balls came to Lucy's mind, and she knew the truth. 'You pawned it.'

He looked up, frowning. 'What do you know of such things?'

'I've been learning,' Lucy said bleakly. It wasn't the kind of knowledge she would have gained had she still been at Miss Martin's, but it was useful in its way. 'Papa,' she added, 'have you had anything to eat?'

Jeremy shook his head. 'It doesn't matter.' He seemed utterly crushed, and Lucy knew he must already have lost the money for the flute.

Without further words, she went downstairs to the kitchen. She had eaten her own supper earlier, but she said to Ada, 'I want two sausages, please, and some bread. It's for my father.'

'Who's going to pay for it?' Ada demanded.

'I am. As soon as I get my wages.' Lucy was quietly blazing with fury, and Ada shrugged and gave her what she asked for.

Upstairs, her father was sitting where she had left him, but he looked up as the smell of the sausages reached him, and Lucy saw how hungry he was.

She watched him while he ate, and when he had finished, she put out her hand and said, 'Please, Papa, give me the pawn ticket.'

He stared at her in outrage. 'I wouldn't dream—'

'Please.' The gaze of her fair-haired mother from the locket in its hiding-place was in Lucy's mind and gave her strength. She had put her own hair up today with the pins and tortoiseshell comb her grandmother had sent, and knew she looked older.

Her father fumbled in his waistcoat pocket and produced a crumpled slip of paper. 'You may as well throw it away,' he said. Then, as if in unbearable weariness, he lay down on his side, facing away from her.

Lucy went back to her half of the room on the other side of the curtain, and looked at the pawn ticket.

Silver flute, 4s. 9d. advanced.

Very quietly, she slid her treasure box from under her bed. Winterthorn's money was still safe in its envelope. *Bellman 5s. 6d.* That was more than enough to get the flute back.

But it's Papa's money, not mine, Lucy thought. Would he want her to use it for this purpose? And if she did, wouldn't the same thing happen again? She sat with the envelope in her hands, wondering what to do. If she asked him, he would take the money from her, as he had every right to do, and then it would be lost and the flute would never come back. And without it, he was not his real self. All the same—

Lucy laid the envelope down on her bed and went to look at her father, with half a mind to let him decide. He was deeply asleep.

'Five bob to pay,' said the pawnbroker.

'But the ticket says four and ninepence!' Lucy objected.

'Interest, fourpence in the pound per month. I'm letting you off a penny as it is, since it only came in today. Do you want the flute or don't you?'

'Yes.' There was no choice.

She headed for the door with the shabby black case under her arm, then turned back. 'Have you got an envelope?'

The man stared at her. 'What d'you mean?'

'I need an envelope, it's very important.'

'Got a cheek, you have.' But he fished under the counter. 'This do?'

'Thank you very much.' The envelope was dog-eared and slightly grubby, but that didn't matter. Lucy gave the man a small curtsy of gratitude, and left the shop. Since he had let her off a penny, perhaps it was reasonable to spend a penny of Papa's money on a stamp.

She let herself in through the back door with the flute hidden underneath her shawl, wanting no questions about where she had been or what she was carrying. Tom was in the kitchen, sitting by the wall on his own. She went to join him.

'Is Finn out?' she asked quietly, and he nodded. Someone was playing a concertina in the corner, and the room was noisy, but there was still a risk that they might be overheard. Lucy and Tom exchanged a glance, then moved into the empty passage that led to the hall.

'They went out about an hour ago,' Tom said. 'Slip and the Duke and Finn. I'll wait up until they come back. What about you? Where have you been?'

Lucy explained about the flute, and Tom listened carefully and didn't interrupt. At the end of it, he sighed. 'I wish we could find somewhere else to live,' he said. 'Just the three of us, you and me and Finn.'

75

'Yes,' said Lucy. It was a fairy-tale idea. 'I'd have to bring Papa as well,' she said. There was nobody else to look after him.

Tom turned away to the kitchen and didn't answer.

Upstairs, Jeremy was still asleep. He did not move when Lucy quietly put the flute down at the foot of his bed, and she was glad. The explanations could wait until tomorrow.

When Lucy came into the kitchen from the yard with an empty bucket the next morning, the Duke caught at her arm from where he sat at the table, eating bread and jam.

'You a pretty girl?' he asked with his mouth full.

Nobody had ever asked her such a question. Lucy blushed and said, 'I don't know.'

'Is she?' the Duke demanded of anyone listening. Slip and several others laughed, and there was a chorus of agreement. 'Stunning!' 'A right beauty!'

'That's what I thought,' said the Duke. 'People like a pretty girl—they buy more.' He gave Lucy's arm a squeeze. 'You can be my guide, girl.'

'But I can't!' Lucy cast about in panic for an excuse. 'I have to help Ada.'

Ada overheard. 'You can do that as well,' she said. 'He never goes out until ten or more—plenty of time to get the morning jobs done first.'

'But . . . George is his guide!'

'Not no more he ain't,' said the Duke. 'He's a goner. Snuffed it yesterday. Them Bible women came round to say.'

'Oh, poor George!'

The Duke was unmoved. 'Better off dead,' he said. 'That boy weren't no more use than a wet kipper.'

Daisy was listening, wearing a grubby dressing gown

76

and sipping a cup of tea. She nudged Lucy and said, 'Tell him you want double the money, love. Can't do two jobs for the price of one.'

'You mind your own business,' said Ada.

Lucy was thinking fast. Winterthorn had promised her half a crown a week, but he would keep the rent of two shillings out of it. That left exactly sixpence for her and Papa to live on through the week—impossible. She owed Ada more than that for food already. 'I want sixpence a day,' she said boldly.

The Duke turned his blank china gaze in her direction and said heavily, 'You will have your little joke. Threepence, and call yourself lucky.'

'Fourpence,' said Lucy. 'And a free supper for me and Papa.'

'I ain't employing your pa,' said the Duke. 'He can find his own supper. And if you're getting fourpence a day and your keep, you'd better be worth it, girl. Do as you're told and no argument, right? I'll want you down here in half an hour, ready to go out.'

Lucy hardly hesitated. 'Right,' she said, and picked up the bucket again.

Her father caught her on the stairs.

'Lucy,' he whispered. 'Where did you get the money?'

It was the question she had been dreading—and with the Duke waiting in the kitchen, there wasn't much time to answer it. She blurted out the truth about Winterthorn's payment for the furniture, and saw the muscles at the side of her father's face tighten with suppressed anger.

He took a deep breath. 'I know you meant well,' he said. 'But you must never, ever, take it upon yourself to do such a thing again.' He grabbed her arm, almost as hard as the Duke had done. 'Don't you see,' he whispered fiercely, 'you robbed me of what might have been the best chance of my life?'

77

'But, Papa,' Lucy said, 'it might *not* have been the best.'

He made a wordless sound of impatience, releasing her with a dismissive gesture. 'You don't understand,' he said. 'Your mother was the same.' He sighed. 'The female mind cannot encompass great possibilities.'

Lucy wondered in a detached sort of way why she was not more upset. As little as a week ago, she would have been reduced to misery by his coldness, but she understood him better now. The notion of greatness and easy riches had devoured her father as mistletoe devours the apple tree, reducing it to a crumbling rottenness. She watched him as he stumbled away down the stairs with the flute in its case in his hand, and could say nothing.

Ten minutes later, Tom came out to find Lucy in the yard, where she was washing the last of the buckets under the pump. He looked white-faced and exhausted.

'Finn never came home,' he said. 'I waited up all night. I don't know where he is, they won't tell me.'

'But what did they *say*?' Lucy was horrified.

'Just that he's all right, I don't have to worry. But I don't trust them. They'd say that anyway, wouldn't they? To shut me up.'

'Oh, Tom—what can we do?'

'Nothing,' said Tom bitterly. 'That's the worst of it.'

Ada's voice rang out from the back door. 'You, Lucy, get in here right now!'

Lucy picked up her bucket. 'I've got to go out with the Duke,' she said, and put her hand on Tom's arm. 'Don't worry. Maybe I can find out something.'

'Be careful,' said Tom.

There was no need for the warning.

78

*   *   *

To her surprise, Lucy found a kind of satisfaction in being the blind man's guide. Despite the weight of his heavy grip on her shoulder, it was better than being shouted at by Ada, who so plainly enjoyed giving the orders now. Out here in the streets, Lucy was in charge of the big man who shuffled half a pace behind her, and she liked the feeling of having a proper job to do. It put her on the same level as the market traders and costermongers, people who earned a living from their own work.

The Duke knew his way amazingly well. As one street led to another, he would tell her, 'Left here,' or, 'Over the road and along the alley.' He let her keep him clear of potholes and rubbish and stop him at the crossings until there was a gap between the cabs and carriages, but he always knew where he was going. When they came to the street market, he halted in a gap between the fish stall and a seller of tin nutmeg graters. 'This is my pitch,' he said.

From the deep pockets of his coat he produced a small tray which he hung round his neck by its string, then several bundles of matches rolled together in a piece of rag. He laid some of them out on the tray with deft fingers, then wrapped the rest up and pushed them back in his pocket. The matches were joined together by the pink stuff of their striking heads in rows of twenty.

'Cigar fuzees,' he bawled at the crowd. 'Strike anywhere, no need for sandpaper. Best quality, straight from Germany, three rows a penny.'

Lucy wondered why he bothered to sell such cheap goods. At three rows a penny, he didn't seem likely to make much money. She wondered uneasily if he would keep his promise to pay her fourpence a day. But the trade was much brisker than she expected. Nine people had bought matches—or 'fuzees', as he called them—in the first hour, and a good few of the Duke's acquaintances had stopped for a word with him. Sometimes it was just to eye Lucy and compliment him on his new guide, but once or twice there would be a muttered conversation that she couldn't catch, and wasn't meant to.

Suddenly the Duke asked her, 'Do you sing?'

'Not very well,' said Lucy. She had heard ladies singing with wonderfully loud, confident voices when she had been with her papa to musical evenings at which he was playing, and knew she couldn't make that kind of sound.

'Didn't ask if you sang well,' said the Duke. 'That's for me to decide. Go on, give us a tune. "The Widow's Last Prayer".'

Nervously, Lucy began to sing.

'Louder.' The blind man reached under her shawl and took a painful pinch of skin just above her elbow.

'Ow!' Lucy stopped singing and tried to pull away, but he was too strong for her.

'Sing louder, then,' he said in her ear. 'I know about music, girl. Had dozens of singers through my hands, I have. Dozens. Taught 'em all they know. You sing loud, you won't get hurt.'

Desperately, Lucy started again, making as much sound as she could, and he nodded. 'That's better.' But his hand remained in place, and whenever her voice slackened its volume, the grip of his fingers tightened.

People stopped to listen, and when Lucy's song ended, the Duke begged, 'Spare a penny for the child.' His white gaze turned skyward as he held out a hopeful palm, and he nudged Lucy with the other elbow, muttering, 'Stick your hand out.'

Lucy did as she was told, and at once a woman gave her a ha'penny.

By mid-day, she had earned fivepence farthing, all of

it transferred to the Duke's pocket, and her voice was cracking and hoarse. 'My throat hurts,' she said, almost in tears.

'Cup of tea, you need,' said the Duke. 'Set you to rights. Know the coffee stall, up by the Punch and Judy?'

'Yes.' She didn't, but it would be easy to find.

'We'll go there.' He rolled up the unsold matches and put them into his pocket, together with the tray.

At the stall, the Duke bought a meat pie for himself and a slice of bread for Lucy, with the promised tea. When they had finished, he said, 'Now we'll try the houses.'

Lucy had no idea what this meant, and she didn't ask. She had been up since half past five, her throat was sore, and she had no energy to waste in talking.

The Duke directed her out of the market and across street after street until they left the crowded rows of buildings behind and came to the big houses that stood in their own grounds, backing onto open country. Each had a driveway that led, Lucy guessed, to stables at the back. Once or twice, she had been to tea at such a house, invited by one of the girls at school. They turned in through the gate of the first one and crunched across the gravel.

'There's steps up to the front door,' Lucy said.

'We'll go up, then,' said the Duke as if it was obvious.

'But—' There had been a notice on the wrought-iron gate, NO BEGGARS, NO HAWKERS. And they were hawking matches, weren't they?

'You arguing?' said the Duke.

'No.' Lucy's arm was already bruised from his punishing grip. She guided him up to the front door.

'Ring the bell,' he said, then added in a low voice, 'and use your eyes.'

A maid in a white cap and apron came to the door and looked alarmed at the sight of them. 'Oh, no,' she said before the Duke had said a word. 'Didn't you see the notice?'

'I can't see anything, my dear,' the Duke told her pathetically. 'Blinded in the service of my country. And my granddaughter here never learned to read; we didn't have the money for schooling. Hard enough with the bringing-up of her after her parents died, poor mite, smallpox it was, and us just finished with six of our own. This one nearly died of the pox as well, but we pulled her through, God be praised, didn't we, darling?' His fingers dug into Lucy's shoulder and she nodded dumbly, too astonished by the mad tale to speak. 'Fuzees for the kitchen, my dear?' he added to the servant. 'Three rows for a penny, you'll never do better.'

'I don't buy things,' the maid said. 'I've got to go, sorry.'

'Of course, my dear, of course,' the Duke ran on. 'No hard feelings at all, it's a pleasure talking to—' The door was shut in his face before he'd finished.

'Well?' he said to Lucy as she guided him down the steps. 'What did you see?'

'She had a cold sore,' Lucy said. 'And she—'

'Not the girl, stupid, the house. What was in the hall? Pictures on the walls, good carpets, silver?'

Lucy took a scared glance at his blank-eyed face and understood. She was not here to help the Duke sell matches, but to spy out which houses were worth robbing. Like Finn, she was being used by thieves. But she dared not let him see that she knew this.

'It was a bit dark in the hall,' she said, trying hard to be helpful. 'I think there was a hat-stand.'

Without warning, the Duke slapped her hard across the face, knocking her sideways. 'You got eyes,' he roared. 'It's your job to see. What am I paying you for?' He gripped her by the shoulder again, pushing her along in front of him as she sobbed with shock. Then he slackened pace, and when he spoke again, his voice was as wheedling as the tone he had used to the housemaid.

'I used to be an artist, you know that? Painted beautiful pictures.' His hand left her shoulder for a moment to sketch in the air. 'People came from miles around, rich men wanting me to paint their wives and their horses and carriages. You ever been in that big gallery in Trafalgar Square?'

'No,' said Lucy.

'Thought not. There's pictures of mine in there, worth a mint. But I got knocked over, see, trying to stop a runaway horse. Caught a hoof across my head, lost my sight. Couldn't paint no more.' He sighed heavily. 'Just think what that's like for an artist. I let the last of my pictures go for nothing, just to pay the rent. I always think I might find one of my portraits in these big houses, that's why I need you to look for me. I'd buy them back, fair and square. Got dealers all over the world wanting them. Are we near another house?'

'We've passed two,' said Lucy, not caring whether he minded or not. Her cheek was stinging, and she didn't believe he'd been an artist.

'None of your lip.' The Duke felt his way through another gate. 'Up the steps, girl. And try harder this time, right?'

A footman in silk stockings and a blue and yellow livery looked at them with disgust. 'Go away at once,' he said. 'The mistress is expecting visitors and she will not want riff-raff like you on the doorstep.'

'Your mistress may have heard of me,' said the Duke. 'Marmaduke van Rubens, famous painter until I lost my sight. She might have one of my pictures.'

'Rubbish,' said the footman, and shut the door.

'Well?' the Duke asked as they made their way back down the drive.

'There was a mirror with a gilt frame above the hall-stand,' Lucy said reluctantly, 'and a picture of a lady with a fan and a little dog.'

'Anything else?'

'A table with a silver tray for people to leave their cards.'

'That's better,' said the Duke.

They moved on again. Lucy stared at the open fields beyond the backs of the houses, and wished she was somewhere else.

8

It was getting dark by the time they came back, and the lamplighter was going from post to post, starting up the small gas flames that blossomed into warm pools of brightness. As Lucy made her way along the street with the Duke beside her, she could hear shouting. Then she realized it was coming from outside their house, where a group of people had gathered to watch what was going on. Her father was in the centre of it, pinned against the front door by a man who was bawling in his face.

Lucy tried to break into a run, but the Duke's heavy hand on her shoulder held her back. 'No, you don't,' he said. She watched in horror as the man went on shouting.

'Where's my money, Bellman? No use telling me you're bankrupt, you don't get out of it that way.' People yelled and whistled agreement. 'You're still walking round the streets like a fine gentleman,' the man went on, 'while honest tradesmen whistle for their money. I'm going to give you in charge, I am—you should be behind bars.'

There were cheers from the crowd, and a voice yelled, 'Wouldn't be the first time!'

Quite near to Lucy, one woman said to another, 'He did ten months in the Marshalsea a while back.'

'What for?' asked her friend.

'Same thing—owing money all round the place. And that was twelve years ago or more. He hasn't changed.' And the pair of them folded their arms and clucked disapprovingly.

The front door of the house was opened by Ada, and

Jeremy bolted past her like a rabbit into its burrow. The crowd yelled and booed.

'Have *you* been paid?' a woman shouted.

Ada put her fists on her hips. 'That's my business,' she said. 'But he won't be here much longer, I tell you that.' Then she went in and banged the door.

'Round the back,' the Duke said in Lucy's ear, and gave her a push. She stumbled down the muddy alleyway that led to the gate into the yard with the blind man treading behind her. Once in the kitchen, she left the Duke talking to Ada and ran for the stairs.

She had only reached the hall when the front door was opened from outside. Lucy halted in sudden terror that the crowd had broken in—but it was Albert Apps, tucking his key into his waistcoat pocket with his usual neatness. The relief of seeing that it was only him made her gasp and put her hands to her face, and Albert frowned in concern.

'I am so sorry about the occurrence outside,' he said. He still sounded like a lawyer's clerk, despite his sympathy. 'I waited at a distance until it was over.'

'Oh, Mr Apps, they can't put Papa in prison, can they?' Lucy blurted.

Albert looked unhappy. 'It's a stupid law,' he said as if to himself. 'Imprisonment benefits nobody in these cases.'

He had answered her question. Lucy turned away in despair—then she looked back at him. 'They said Papa had been in prison before. Is that true?' It was better to know.

'I was not living here at the time,' Albert said evasively, then changed the subject. 'What about the little boy— Tom's brother? Is he back yet?'

'I don't think so. I haven't seen Tom since this morning.' Lucy was startled. How did Mr Apps know Finn was missing? She didn't think he had any contact with the kitchen people.

'I wondered if I should make some enquiries into his whereabouts,' Albert said, 'though I understand the matter is . . . a little delicate.'

'You mustn't!' Lucy thought of Tom's frantic response when she had suggested asking her father to help. 'Please, Mr Apps, don't!'

Albert sighed. 'Such a dilemma,' he said, 'but one really should try to do the right thing.' Again, he was not really speaking to Lucy. He was a man who had lived alone for many years, and talked more easily to himself than to anyone else.

'I must go to Papa,' Lucy said, and Albert was all courteous attention again.

'Yes, of course. Please give him my kind regards.' He stood back to let Lucy go up the stairs ahead of him.

Jeremy was sitting on his bed, staring at nothing. Lucy sat down beside him, and after a moment he asked in a low voice, 'You heard them? Those people outside—what they said?'

'Yes, Papa.'

He sighed. 'I was afraid so. I saw you there, with the blind man.' He looked at her in despair. 'What can you think of me?'

Lucy tried hard to keep her voice steady. 'You are my very dear father,' she said. 'Always.'

Jeremy made a little sound that wasn't quite a laugh. 'That's more than I deserve,' he said.

After a few moments, Lucy asked, 'When did it happen, Papa?'

Jeremy sat back and sighed again. Then he began to speak, and, like Albert Apps, his words sounded as if he had said them often to himself.

'If only Elizabeth hadn't died. I was doing well as a

musician, playing at concerts and soirées, giving lessons. There were so many more people to pay after she was gone. Nursemaid, housekeeper, laundry-woman—' He looked at Lucy with an apologetic shrug. 'I've never been good at managing money. Your mother used to do all that. But afterwards—I couldn't make enough through the music. I thought I should concentrate on the shop.'

'That was a good idea,' Lucy said, but her father was caught up in his own words, telling at last the story he had carried for so long.

'It was quite high-class at first, not like it is now. Maybe I aimed too high—this isn't a rich district. I borrowed money to buy in the stock, but it didn't sell fast enough to cover the repayments. Then I was lucky with a horse race, and for a little while things were better. But it didn't last. My suppliers became impatient, they wouldn't wait. They had me arrested for debt. I was in prison for the best part of a year.' His eyes met Lucy's, frowning. 'You wouldn't remember, you were very small. Your grandmother took you at the time.'

So Grandma knows all about it, Lucy thought. She waited for her father to go on.

'Winterthorn came to see me in prison. That's when he offered me a mortgage on the house. The terms weren't good, but it was my only chance, so I took it. Your grandmother wanted me to leave you with her, she said she'd bring you up. But how could I do that?' He reached for her hand. 'You are all I have, Lucy. The only thing to live for. If only luck had been kinder.'

A small protest rose in Lucy's mind. *If Papa had not looked for luck all the time, things might have been better*. But it would be unkind to say this now. 'You could give music lessons again,' she suggested. At least the flute was still there beside her father's bed.

Jeremy glanced round the attic room and gave a hopeless shrug. 'In this hovel?'

'You said you'd go to other people's houses.' But Lucy saw how different he looked now. She remembered him as assured and well-groomed, but he had become shabby. His hair was uncut and straggling, and his clothes were threadbare. Worse still, he had lost all belief in himself. He was as helpless in the tide of luck as a scrap of paper washed down a muddy gutter after a rainstorm.

She stood up. 'I'll get us some food,' she said, with no fear of having to argue with Ada. After her day with the Duke, she had earned more than enough to pay for it.

In the hall, Alfred Apps was talking to Ada, and his voice sounded agitated. Lucy drew back, waiting at the top of the first flight of stairs until they had finished.

'I know the law,' Albert was insisting. 'There are severe penalties for abducting children, and I have reason to believe that young Finn has been removed from this house against his will, quite possibly to be forced into criminal activities. I have thought about this carefully, and realize there may be a risk to the person who informed me about what is going on, but my duty is plain. If the child is not returned here, safe and unharmed, within twenty-four hours, I shall go to the police.'

Lucy smothered a silent gasp. This could be terribly dangerous for Finn.

Ada was shouting at Albert. 'You do that! You just do that, and see what you get. They'll never believe you, anyway. You don't know what you're talking about, you'll look a fool.'

'I don't think so,' said Albert calmly. 'I bid you good evening, Miss Clegg.' And Lucy heard him coming up the stairs. She started down the flight as if she was simply on her way to the kitchen and had not overheard, but as they passed, Albert gave her a small, deliberate nod. 'It had to be done,' he said quietly. Then he went on up, with the line of his droopy moustache set in a new determination.

Lucy ducked into the shop. 'Tom, listen—someone's told Mr Apps about Finn, and he's threatened Ada with going to the police. I just heard him.'

Tom looked up from folding a pile of second-hand vests, and his face was aghast. 'How did he know?'

'It wasn't me that told him, honest,' Lucy said. 'I never breathed a word to Papa or anyone.'

Tom groaned and shut his eyes. 'This is just what I was afraid of.' Then he was practical again. 'Get into the kitchen, Lucy, quickly. Try to pick up any hint you can about what they're going to do. I've got to find out where Finn is—just got to.'

In the hot kitchen, Ada looked round from where she was whispering to the Duke, and scowled when she saw Lucy. 'I'm surprised you've got the cheek to show your face in here,' she said. 'Tittle-tattling round the place.'

'What d'you mean?' Lucy managed to sound astonished and hurt. Everyone in the kitchen had stopped talking, and she knew every word she said was being listened to.

'Gossiping to that layabout Tom,' said Ada. 'His brother's being well taken care of, like we told him.'

Lucy frowned as if she was puzzled. 'Course he is,' she agreed. 'Did anyone say he wasn't?' She hoped her gaze was convincingly innocent.

Ada looked at her suspiciously. 'Someone's said so. There's a lot of lies being told, and when I find out who's been telling them, there'll be trouble.'

'Well, it wasn't me,' said Lucy.

For a dreadful moment she thought her act hadn't worked, then Ada shrugged and turned away. 'I suppose you want your supper.'

'Yes, please,' said Lucy. 'And for Papa as well.' Talk began in the room again, but she knew she must not relax yet. Any sigh of relief or hint of a private smile would give the game away. *They've got to think I don't understand anything.*

Ada forked two fried herrings onto plates and added some cabbage and hunks of bread. 'Get back down here, soon as you've finished that,' she said, 'and hurry up.'

'All right.' Lucy went out with her two plates, still being careful to look like a girl who was too young and inexperienced to know anything about how the real world worked.

On her way up the last flight of stairs, Lucy paused. The sound of the flute was coming from the attic room, and she heard it strangely, as if for the first time. She had listened to her father play from her earliest childhood, but now it gave her a sense of painful pride that her papa could create this music. She had been so afraid he would pawn the instrument again, but he had not, and she was touched by that.

Jeremy was playing a quiet lament, a slow tune with little breaks and turns in between its long phrases, and gooseflesh bloomed on Lucy's arms and down the back of her neck as she stood outside the door with the plates in her hands. *Papa has his own world*, she thought. And for all its lack of reason and its crazy dreams, it was beautiful and worth defending.

'Right,' said Ada when Lucy went back to the kitchen. 'You're in charge here. Herrings are a penny each, with cabbage and bread another penny. Ale twopence a pint, and they're not to help themselves. I'll be upstairs, and don't come pestering.'

Lucy promised she wouldn't. Looking round the room, she saw that the only people there were strangers who came to get a bed for the night. The Duke wasn't at the table any more, and neither was Slip or the red-haired man or any of Ada's friends. *They're all upstairs,* she thought, *deciding what to do about Finn.* But that was as far as her imagination went. When she thought about Tom's little brother, she met a blank in her mind which no amount of wondering could fill.

Tom came in. Lucy gave him an extra herring and told him about the meeting going on upstairs.

'I know who told Mr Apps,' Tom said as he ate. 'A couple of girls came into the shop just now with Daisy—one of them bought a pair of boots. They were the same sort of girls—you know what I mean.'

Lucy nodded.

'They were talking among themselves and laughing,' Tom went on, 'and one of them said to Daisy, "Nice for you being in the same house as Albert now. Nice for him, too—just down the stairs and into your room." And Daisy turned pink and told her to shut up.'

'Oh, Tom! Mr *Apps*? I can't believe it!' Albert was so courteous and respectable. Surely he wouldn't—'Maybe they're just friends.'

'Doesn't matter what they are,' said Tom. 'She's the one who told him about Finn.' He shrugged. 'But it doesn't help.'

Lucy's father played for a long time that night, as if, having started, he could not bear to stop. As she used to when she was a child—so long ago, it seemed now—Lucy fell asleep with her mind and heart full of music.

The next day seemed ordinary enough. Lucy was up before dawn as usual to light the stove and wash last night's dishes, sweep the hall and stairs and empty the dreadful buckets. Then she went out with the Duke.

Fog lay heavy over the river and drifted round the

market stalls, added to by the steaming breath of men and horses and the hot smoke of roasting chestnuts. Street traders coughed and beat their arms across their chests, and the barefoot children who sold watercress had spangles of moisture in their matted hair as they held up their green bunches and piped, 'Two for a ha'penny—who'll buy?'

The rawness of the wet air caught at Lucy's throat and made singing difficult, but the Duke did not pinch her arm when her voice broke into a cough. 'Cup of tea you need, girl,' he said helpfully.

From one coffee stall they went to another, the Duke chatting amiably to his cronies with no intention of any more selling or singing as far as Lucy could see. By mid-afternoon they were in an ale-house, and the Duke was still keeping up an almost theatrical performance of being very nice. He talked to any stranger who would listen, and his rambling stories sounded so much like the fancies of a harmless old man that Lucy found her fear of him starting to abate a little. *After all*, she told herself, *the poor man is blind. How would I like it?*

Sitting in the warm, beery-smelling room, Lucy stared through the window at the gas lamps that were beginning to twinkle in the early dusk, and then at the red face of the serving woman and the bright reflections of firelight glinting on bottles and mugs. She knew how lost she would feel if these things were replaced by unchanging darkness. Her pity for the Duke started to grow quite strong—but then she thought of little Finn, hidden somewhere in the hugger-mugger of alleys and close-packed houses, perhaps among people who would not care if he was hurt or frightened. No, she must not relax her guard.

It was late when they returned. The house stood with its front door open, and Lucy was relieved to see that no crowd stood outside tonight. People were entering in ones

93

and twos, to pay their money to Ada for a night's lodging, but everything seemed quiet. As she guided the Duke up the step, Ada glanced at him and said casually, 'All right?'

'Fine,' said the Duke. 'Couldn't be better.'

Among the waiting people was a young man who seemed different from the others. He wore an ordinary cap and a jacket with a muffler tucked into the neck, but his hands were very clean, and he held a pair of yellowish leather gloves. He stood back a little from the queue which had formed, as if waiting to speak to Ada privately, and his round, pink face wore an expression of concern.

'Yes?' said Ada when she had dealt with the others. 'Can I help you?'

'My name is William Jinks,' the young man said. 'I am employed by Brisket and MacFarden, solicitors. I believe Albert Apps lives here.'

'He does,' agreed Ada. 'What of it?'

'I just wondered if he was ill,' said William Jinks. 'He works for our firm, you see, but he didn't arrive this morning. Mr Brisket asked if I would enquire. Albert's never missed a day before, not in seventeen years.'

Ada's face did not change. 'Far as I know, he went to work as usual,' she said. 'But I'm busy in the mornings, I never see him go out.' She gave Lucy a smile. 'Did you see Mr Apps go out this morning?'

'No,' said Lucy. Uneasiness was settling somewhere round her heart, but she was trying to push it away. *He's all right. He must be all right.*

'And I didn't see him,' said the Duke. 'But then, I don't see anything.' He smiled as well, turning his blank stare on the young man.

'I wonder—could someone go and look?' asked William Jinks. 'I'm sorry to be a nuisance, but Mr Brisket said—'

'Course you can,' said the Duke. 'Lucy here will show you his room, won't you, girl?' And his hand on her shoulder tightened its grip.

Lucy nodded wordlessly.

'Take the spare key,' Ada said helpfully, fishing in her pocket. 'He locks up when he goes out—he's the careful sort, isn't he?'

Going up the stairs with the pink-faced young man behind her, Lucy knew she would find the room empty. She could understand now why the Duke had been so cheerful all day. He and his friends had dealt with Albert's threat to tell the police, and it didn't trouble them any more. They had taken him away, just as they had taken Finn, to some secret hiding place. But where was it? How could she and Tom find out? With her mind full of these problems, Lucy tapped at the door. There was silence as she expected, so she turned the key in the lock and looked in.

The room was dark, with its heavy curtains closed across the windows. It was very cold, and smelt faintly of kippers.

'Mr Apps?' William Jinks asked. The silence continued, so he made his way carefully across the carpet and pulled a curtain aside to let in the light of the street lamp. And then Lucy saw Albert.

He was spreadeagled in the leather armchair by the cold, ashy fire. His legs were sprawled across the hearthrug and his head lay back over the arm of the chair, with his open eyes staring at the ceiling. His neck looked as long and white as that of a plucked chicken, and even in the dimness, the dark bruising on either side of his windpipe was clearly visible.

Lucy pressed her hands tightly over her mouth, but a high, terrified scream was filling the room, and for a few moments she could not believe it was coming from herself.

People were running up the stairs, pushing past her into the room. She was being jostled, and there was a confusion of voices.

'What's happened?'

'By the fire, look.'

'Oh, my God, it's Mr Apps.'

'Mind out of the way.' Ada pushed past, holding a lit candle high. She stared down at Albert, then she turned and looked across the room at Lucy, who still stood by the door. 'I know whose work this was,' she said in a loud, clear voice. 'Your pa's always hated Albert. They've nearly come to blows many a time, over that blessed flute.'

Lucy was sobbing uncontrollably. She blundered her way out, and William Jinks was behind her. 'I'm going to get the police,' he said, but Lucy was running up the stairs to her attic room and hardly heard him.

Jeremy was not there. Lucy stood inside the door, trembling and shuddering. She felt chilled to the bone by the coldness of the room downstairs where Albert lay sprawled in his ugly death. She sat on her bed, hugging herself as she wept, but there was no warmth in her own thin arms.

After what seemed hours, a soft tap sounded at the door. 'Lucy?'

'Oh, Tom!'

He came in and sat beside her, then took both her hands. 'Are you all right?'

Lucy nodded, but her teeth were chattering. She managed to say, 'You'll have to go back to the shop.'

He shook his head. 'The police are here,' he told her. 'The shop's closed. Nobody's to go in or out of the house.'

'But Papa's not back yet!'

'Yes, he is. Downstairs.' Tom looked uneasy. 'The police are talking to him. Ada's saying your father didn't

96

like Albert because Albert complained about him playing the flute. She says he was playing last night, and there was an argument.'

'But there wasn't! It's not true!'

'I know. But that's their story, and they're all sticking to it.'

Lucy stared into Tom's troubled grey eyes, and things tumbled into place with terrible clarity. They hadn't just taken Albert away to stop him going to the police about Finn, they'd killed him. And her father was to take the blame. 'I must go and see him,' she said.

In the next moment she was running down the stairs, first one flight then the next—but a few steps from the hall, she stopped. Two policemen were escorting her father out into the street. He turned his pale face to her and opened his mouth as if to say something, then he was hidden from her sight as the door was shut.

Lucy rushed to it, but Ada blocked her way.

'You, get in the kitchen,' she said. 'Everyone's waiting for their supper.'

'I won't,' Lucy raged, 'I'm never going in there again, I—'

Ada shook her hard by both arms, and her face was close to Lucy's as she hissed, 'Listen, young miss. You'd best be careful.'

Lucy shut her eyes and freed a hand to put it over her eyes as the truth sank in. If these people had killed Albert to protect their secrets, they could kill her, too. She took a shuddering breath. 'All right,' she said.

'That's better.' And Ada stood back to let her make her way to the kitchen.

9

The next day, Lucy could not sing. Despite the Duke's grip on her elbow, she kept thinking of her father and of poor Albert, and she found herself in tears.

'Crying won't do you no good,' the Duke said. 'Come on, girl, cheer up.'

Lucy shook her head. Even speaking was difficult. 'Things are just . . . awful.'

'Depends how you look at it,' said the Duke.

'How *can* I look at it?' She was suddenly furious. 'Mr Apps has been killed and Papa is in prison, and I don't understand anything.' She scrubbed at her eyes with her sleeve, angry with herself as well. She should not be talking to this man, who was so much part of all the things she feared and mistrusted.

The Duke gave a bark of laughter. 'Turn a blind eye, girl,' he said, 'same as I do. That's three blind eyes between us, one of yours and two of mine. We'll be all right, long as you don't do nothing silly. What the eye don't see, the heart don't grieve over. You want to remember that.'

There was an edge of menace to his words although they sounded consoling, and Lucy thought of what Ada had said last night. *You'd best be careful.* She could not fight these people—they were too strong.

'Coffee stall,' said the Duke.

So this was to be another of his good-natured days. Lucy moved forward with the familiar weight of the blind man's hand on her shoulder. *I must think, I must think*. It wasn't easy—her mind felt as scattered as crumbs thrown to birds. One thing stood out. The only way she could help her father was to find out who had really killed Albert. Was it Slip, whose blue-scarred nose made him look so dangerous, or the weasel-faced man with the red hair? It was impossible to say—there were so many furtive, grubby people in and out of the kitchen now. But if Lucy tried to stand out against them, she would be told nothing, and quite possibly she, too, might disappear into some dark hiding place, or be found dead like Mr Apps.

She stared down at the mud between the cobblestones as she walked on with the Duke at her side. The only chance was to pretend she wanted to be one of the gang. But would they believe it, after she had been so angry and upset? Why should they? She'd have to do something very convincing.

An idea began to take shape. She would have to make out that she believed her father had killed Albert. The idea was a dreadful one—but if she could imagine she really had lost faith in him, it would give her a natural excuse to turn to the kitchen people. There was nobody else. They would have to become her family.

Lucy went on thinking about it as they reached the coffee stall. Because she'd been brought up in such a protected way, the Duke and the others might believe she would turn to them, being helpless on her own. And it was almost true. She had nowhere else to live but in the house that now belonged to Winterthorn, and no way to make any money except through the work provided by Ada and the Duke.

Warming her hands round a hot mug of tea, she frowned down into its steam. She would have to take the first step, right now. She cleared her throat and started to ask, 'Do you think Papa really—'

She could not go on, even in pretence, but the Duke gave a satisfied chuckle. 'No doubt about it, girl,' he said. 'That's why he's in Newgate. He'll stand trial for murder. Don't you worry, though. You'll be all right with us.' He turned his sightless gaze to the woman behind the copper urn. 'I'll have a nice, big slice of plum-cake, Betsy,' he said. 'For my granddaughter here.' And he patted Lucy on the shoulder.

The woman raised her eyebrows as she glanced at the pair of them, but she said nothing. And neither did Lucy.

'Tom,' Lucy said quietly that evening, 'where is Newgate?'

He looked at her, knowing what she meant. 'It's about half an hour's walk. Over the river, not far from St Paul's.'

'I must go and see Papa,' said Lucy. There were still people in the kitchen, but most of them had finished eating.

'I'll come with you,' Tom said.

'Will you really? Could we go now? I know it's late, but I can't go during the day.' Then Lucy thought of Finn. 'Or do you want to stay here in case—'

Tom shook his head. 'Finn won't come back. Not on his own, anyway, I can see that now. If they choose to bring him back, they will.'

And if not . . . He left the words unspoken, and so did Lucy. 'Go out the front way,' she whispered, because Ada was standing by the back door, talking to Slip. Lucy picked up her shawl from where it lay on a bench, and went casually out as if she was going up to her room. After a few moments, Tom followed her. Very quietly, they eased the door open and let themselves out.

The thick, stone walls of Newgate were broken by windows

100

that were hardly more than slits, heavily grated and set just above the level of the street. Lucy thought with horror of her father shut in one of the dark cells that lay inside. She wondered if she would be taken down there to see him, or whether he would be brought up to some visiting room, barred perhaps, where they could talk. She went on with Tom at her side, and reached the entrance to the prison. Worn stone steps led to a closed, narrow door, armoured with iron and topped by heavy spikes at face-level, and the stone lintel above it was carved into the heavy shapes of three sets of fetters. A group of women, some with small children, stood under the lamp outside, talking together. One of them was wiping away tears.

A man in a broad-brimmed leather hat was looking out from between the spikes. Lucy put her question nervously.

'Please, sir, can I see my father?'

'And who may your father be?' He sounded very bored.

'His name's Jeremy Bellman.'

The man turned his head slightly and asked an unseen person, 'Bellman?'

'Remanded for the murder of Albert Apps,' a shout came back.

'But it's all wrong!' Lucy burst out. 'Papa never killed anyone, he wouldn't!'

'That's what they all say.' The man indicated the group under the lamp. 'Just heard the same story from them out there. You're too late, anyway—visiting stopped two hours ago.' Then he added with a flicker of interest, 'You got any money?'

Lucy shook her head.

'Because if you had,' he went on, 'and you was to see me right, I could get a few things for your pa. Some of the prisoners has food sent in from the coffee-house over the road. Jugs of ale, too, tobacco—whatever they want.'

'We'll come back when we're rich,' Tom said angrily, and took Lucy's hand.

'Suit yourself,' said the man as they turned away.

As she and Tom walked back to the house, Lucy was tormented by thoughts of her father on trial in the grand surroundings of some court-house. The lawyers in their wigs and robes would be talking in their long words, and Papa, so thin and shabby among all that richness, could only plead the simple truth, that he had nothing to do with Albert's death.

But the truth might go against him. Her father would admit, because it was true, that Albert had irked him with his complaints about the flute. As soon as he said that, it would fit exactly with Ada's story of an argument between them on the night that Albert was killed.

An even worse thought came. Lucy herself could not be certain where her father was at the time of Albert's death. She had gone to sleep that night to the sound of his playing, but she had no idea what time the music had stopped, and whether her papa had gone anywhere after that. The long days of hard work were exhausting, and Lucy had slept deeply, hearing nothing until Ada banged on her door in the morning. She'd seen that Jeremy was asleep in his bed then, but what had happened in between? Had there in fact been an argument downstairs? If there had, she would never have heard it. *I can't prove he's innocent.* The silent words were clear and bleak in her mind. 'Tom,' she said aloud, 'what am I to do?'

'I don't know.' He sounded wretched. They had reached London Bridge and, without saying anything, they stopped to lean on the parapet, both of them staring out across the dark water with its gleaming reflections of lights from the ships.

'Lucy, I've got to find Finn,' Tom said. 'I can't just stay in the house—I'll have to go and look for him.'

She stared at him. 'But how? Where will you start?'

'Daisy told me something.' He was frowning as he met Lucy's eyes. 'I didn't dare mention it in the house; you never know who's listening. There's a place down by the river that the gang use. Daisy doesn't know where it is exactly, only that it's past the docks, down towards Rotherhithe. She's heard them talking about it. They call it Jacob's Island. Finn could be there.'

It would be awful in the house without Tom, Lucy thought. He was her only friend now that Papa was gone—whatever would she do without him? *Don't be selfish*, she scolded herself. Tom was desperately worried about his little brother. And besides, he was right—as long as he stayed in the house and went on working obediently for Ada and the others, he couldn't do anything about Finn. But once he left, he'd never be able to come back.

'If you find Finn,' she said, trying to keep her voice steady, 'what will you do then?'

'Head out of London, I reckon,' Tom said. 'Get a place on a farm, maybe, where we can work. Somewhere safe.' A cab trotted past, and its red tail-lights cast a passing glow over his face as he looked at Lucy. He put his hand on her sleeve. 'I won't forget you, don't worry. I'll get a message to you somehow, then you can come and join us. We'll have our own place, like we always said.'

Lucy nodded. 'One day,' she said. 'Maybe.' Tom's concerns were different from hers. His brother came first. When it came to the task of proving that Jeremy had not killed Albert Apps, Lucy was on her own.

The next morning, Tom was gone.

'Where is he?' Ada raged, shaking Lucy by the shoulder. 'The pair of you sneaked out last night, don't think I don't know. You've been plotting something.'

'He just came with me to try and see my father.' Lucy was glad to be able to tell the truth. 'Only we were too late, so we couldn't. And I don't know where he is, honestly I don't. He didn't say.'

'Huh.' But Ada released her and went back to her normal grumbles. 'What are you hanging about for? The Duke's waiting.'

Lucy had been dreaming all night of pretending to be one of 'the family', and as she guided the blind man through the streets, it seemed even more urgent. With Tom gone, her only hope of finding out any scraps of truth about Albert's murder would be through getting as close as she could to the Duke. She would have to do her best to please him.

All morning, she sang as well as she could, and saw with a kind of satisfaction that people dropped more coins than usual into his outstretched hand. When they went to the coffee stall, she said carefully, 'You're all I've got now. You and Ada and the others.'

'We're all right,' the Duke agreed. 'You want to remember that, girl.'

It couldn't matter to him much whether she remembered it or not, Lucy thought. Perhaps it saved them trouble, though, if she seemed safely on their side. That way, they could be fairly sure she would tell no tales—and it was easier to use her as a servant and guide than go to the bother of getting rid of her. Even to the kitchen people, hiding people and murdering them must be a risky business.

The Duke handed her a hot sausage roll, and Lucy bit into it gratefully. But she mustn't be too grateful, she thought, otherwise she might start trusting him, and that would be a mistake. She had to remember she was not on his side at all. Mr Winterthorn would be coming tonight, and she'd get her week's wages. Tomorrow she would buy some proper paper and an envelope and write again to her grandmother, to tell her what had happened to Papa. There was nothing Grandma could do about it, miles away in Exeter, but at least she would know what was going on. Somebody had to know. *If anything happens to me*— Lucy left the silent words unfinished, but when she spoke to the Duke again, her voice wobbled a bit.

'I've been thinking about Papa. I'm . . . I'm not going to see him again, am I? Ever.' It was too close to the truth to be bearable. The sausage roll seemed impossible to eat, and her eyes swam with sudden tears.

The Duke took a noisy slurp of his tea and said, 'You best forget him. He weren't a bad sort at heart, but you can say the same about a dog with three legs. Never bite you, but it's still got a bit missing. Them as gamble—well, they're no good. All my life,' he added piously, 'I've tried to do good. That's how I lost my sight, trying to rescue a woman and her baby from a fire—did I ever tell you?'

Lucy shook her head, forgetting that he couldn't see her, but the Duke went on without waiting for an answer. 'I used to own this big house in Westminster, see. It was left me by my father. I'd servants and all, carriage and pair, the lot. A footman upset the lamp-oil one night, set the place ablaze. They tried to hold me back—"You can't go in there, sir," they said, "it's a raging inferno." Which it was, girl. But I knew this young housemaid was in there with her baby—she weren't no better than she should be, but that don't matter when it's life or death. So in I went, and this bit of burning timber come right down on top of me. They had to drag me out by my boots. They said I should have got a medal.'

The owner of the coffee stall raised her eyebrows, wiping the counter in a way that showed she didn't believe a word of it, and Lucy almost smiled. But not quite. 'What happened to the woman and her baby?' she asked.

105

'Oh, I'd got 'em out by that time,' said the Duke, draining the last of his tea. 'I'll have a refill, Betsy, thank you.'

'I think that's wonderful,' Lucy said earnestly. Wanting to sound even more appreciative, she added, 'And I think it's right, what we do, going round the houses.'

She knew at once that she'd taken a step too far. The Duke turned his china gaze in her direction, and his voice was suddenly cold. 'And what d'you mean by that?'

'Nothing, really. It's just—' Oh, what a mistake. She'd meant to reassure him that she was on his side, but it had misfired. He knew now that she connected their visits with stealing from the houses. She wasn't supposed to know that. What could she say?

In panic, she remembered Daisy's words, and floundered through them. 'Some people have so much, and there's others who have nothing. It's just luck, really, the way you're born . . . ' Her words tailed away. There was no going back now. 'So if we even it out a bit—I mean, why not?'

'You been talking to someone,' said the Duke. 'Sounds like Daisy to me, she got a lot of funny ideas like that.' He gripped Lucy's arm suddenly. 'Was it Daisy?'

'Well, yes, but it wasn't about you or anything, we were just—'

His fingers dug deeper into her arm. 'I don't like them as talks, girl. Never did.'

'I'm sorry!' Lucy was half-sobbing. 'I only meant—'

'I know what you meant.' The Duke released her with a little push. She felt that his blind gaze was seeing her, although the pale blue centre of the china eye stared away along the street. 'You're all right, girl,' he went on, 'long as you keep your mouth shut. But as to Daisy—I think we'll have to have a little word.'

106

*   *   *

Winterthorn walked into the kitchen that night followed closely by two large men. He stood between these bodyguards in a space by the table where people hastily moved aside to make room for him, and felt in the inside pocket of his ginger coat.

'Wages,' he said. He handed a package to Ada. 'Bellman's rent has been deducted as agreed, so you give his daughter sixpence. Plus whatever else she's earned.' Then he glanced round at the people who were still drinking and eating, and added, 'I would like to speak to those who know me, in private. In the room next door, I suggest.'

A glance ran between Slip and the ginger-haired man, and Ada said, 'Daisy's there.'

'With a client?' asked Winterthorn.

'No, but—'

'Then don't argue.' He led the way, followed by his two henchmen. The others straggled after him, muttering but curious.

Lucy hung back, but the Duke had his hand on her shoulder. 'You, too,' he said.

As people invaded her room, Daisy scrambled off her bed and stood in the far corner, but by the light of the lamp which Ada carried, Lucy saw that the girl's face was swollen and bruised, one eye closed. She was going to call out to her, but Daisy half-raised her hand. *Don't say anything.*

Lucy's own hands covered her face, in shame and horror. Why had she so clumsily tried to tell the Duke she was on his side? He wasn't stupid. He knew she'd never have suspected that thievery went on unless someone had told her. Without Tom's warning, she might have believed his tale about wanting to find the pictures he had painted.

107

The Duke knew that, too. He knew everything. Lucy, in her blundering innocence, had betrayed Daisy and laid her open to this punishment. *A little word*, he'd called it. As if to make sure she was learning the same lesson, the Duke's grip on her shoulder tightened momentarily before he released her. That's why he had brought her in here—to make sure she understood.

'This will not take long,' Winterthorn was saying, and his voice was clipped and angry. 'There will be no argument.' His eye fell on Lucy. 'Miss Bellman, kindly leave the room.'

'Make sure they're not helping themselves to beer,' Ada hissed at her as she passed.

Lucy went back to the kitchen, where a couple of sailors had started to sing a bawdy song to the strains of a concertina. A man was indeed filling his pint mug from the barrel. 'That's tuppence,' she said, and he paid her without argument, rather to her surprise. When she had served everyone else who looked likely to want a drink, she slipped out into the yard. The stink of sewage was very bad now—Ada had told her to throw ashes over the growing pile, but it didn't help. Lucy hoped the night-soil men would be round with their cart on Sunday. Holding her skirt clear of the filth, she made her way to the crack of light that shone between the drawn curtains of Daisy's room, and stood there, listening intently.

'You done all right out of us,' the Duke was saying resentfully. 'Got your cut every time and took none of the risks.'

'And you,' Winterthorn retorted, 'have had a roof over your head and a ready market for any goods purloined. As to myself—' his voice rose a little—'my ridiculously small share of your activities has never been important. It was merely a small amusement. I am above all a businessman, known and respected in society. Your bungling interference in the matter of a tenant whom you found inconvenient has caused me the embarrassment of having policemen on my own doorstep, together with some impertinent lawyer asking questions as if I were a common criminal. This will cause gossip among my neighbours and friends, and I will not tolerate it.'

Slip's voice was raised in objection. 'The Peelers have got Bellman for old Apps—there won't be no more trouble.'

'Sir Robert Peel's police force,' Winterthorn said icily, 'has until now been constrained by public opinion not to come nosing into the affairs of private citizens. However, they are rapidly taking the law into their own hands. I cannot and will not be seen to have anything to do with this mess you have created. I am therefore barring all of you from this house. I'll put in another couple to look after the boarders, and I want the lot of you out by tomorrow at the latest.'

There was a babble of furious talk, and Lucy heard Ada's shrill voice demanding, 'Where are we to go?'

'That is no concern of mine,' Winterthorn said. Then he added more quietly, 'There is an alternative, as we both know.'

The noise was rising, and Winterthorn raised his voice above it. 'I told you, I am not listening to argument. You will be out of here within twenty-four hours. And if there should be any official investigation, I will say you left this house of your own accord and for your own reasons.'

'What if we don't?' a man shouted.

'In that case,' said Winterthorn, 'I shall explain to the police exactly why the unfortunate tenant met his death, and who was responsible for it.'

There was a moment of aghast silence, then a furious outburst of indignation and the sound of a scuffle, followed by a sickening thump and a yell of pain. The bodyguards had moved into action, Lucy realized, and the meeting was obviously about to be over.

She slipped back into the steamy kitchen, where everyone had joined in the singing and nothing could have been heard of the scuffle next door. She was shivering a little from the cold air and from the awful excitement of what she had heard. All else apart, Winterthorn obviously knew who had killed Albert—and it wasn't Papa. Lucy blew on her fingers to warm them, and was innocently serving beer when Winterthorn flung open the door and came through with his two men. He paused when he saw her, and his fox-brown eyes rested on her thoughtfully.

'Miss Bellman,' he said, 'I am making domestic changes in this house, but they need not concern you. I'd be happy to offer you a place on my own staff. Living in, of course.'

For a moment, Lucy hesitated. Could she trust him? She thought of Daisy, who had not known what she was getting herself into until it was too late. There was something about Winterthorn that made her skin prickle with caution, but perhaps she ought to go to his house, because of what he knew. She might find out more there than through staying with the Duke and Ada. She made up her mind.

'Thank you,' she said. 'That's very kind. When should I—'

'Have your things ready tomorrow,' Winterthorn said. 'I'll send for you.'

Lucy dropped a small curtsy, and he went out, with his two human bulldogs following him.

The next morning was weirdly normal. Lucy got up and went about her work as usual, and nobody spoke to her about what had happened. Ada paid her the money owed for a week's work, but when Lucy asked what Winterthorn had meant about 'domestic changes', she snapped, 'Mind your own business.'

'But . . . he said I was to go and work at his house,' said Lucy.

Ada turned away with a lift of her thin eyebrows. She had taken to plucking them lately, sitting at the kitchen table with a pair of tweezers and a hand-mirror.

The Duke said, 'You'll be staying with us, girl. Where you belong.'

Lucy wondered what Winterthorn would say. She had already bundled her few clothes and tied them with string, and the rest of her possessions were under her bed with her treasure box. 'Are we going out?' she asked.

'In a bit,' said Ada. 'Do stop pestering.'

'Sorry—I'll get my shawl.'

In the hall, she paused. Was there enough time to run out and buy an envelope and some paper? No, probably not—and there would be big trouble if Ada found her missing when she was wanted. But Lucy had dreamed all night of Grandma opening a letter from her and reading it to Grandpa, who was still alive and interested, and, today, it seemed vital to make the letter a real thing.

An idea came into her head, so disgraceful that it shocked her. Albert Apps would have had paper. Letters used to come for him quite often, and he must have answered them. She ran up the stairs and paused outside his room. No, she couldn't go in. And yet—would it do any harm? The poor man couldn't write letters now. She opened the door and looked in cautiously, half afraid he would still be sprawled in his chair. He wasn't there, but his furniture stood untouched—his armchair by the fireplace, his tidy bed, his wall cupboard and washstand, and a desk with a closed, sloping lid, over by the window.

Lucy crept across to it, feeling like a thief, and turned the small key. Inside, she found narrow wooden compartments that were filled with neat stacks of letters, some of them tied with dark blue tape. There was paper as well, and envelopes, and even some penny stamps. Because she *wasn't* a thief, Lucy felt in her pocket for money, and put tuppence in the desk. That should be enough, and it didn't matter who would find the coins and use them. She took a sheet of paper, an envelope, and a stamp, closed the desk and fled up the stairs to her room.

With the stub of pencil she had kept in her treasure box, she wrote a quick message to her grandmother.

Dear Grandma,

Mr Apps is dead. Papa has been arrested. He is in Newgate but it was nothing to do with him. I am trying to find out who it was. Please do not worry, I am well, but I think I may be leaving this house. I will write again when I can.

In haste,

Your loving granddaughter,

Lucy

The Duke noticed when she slipped her letter into a pillar box.

'Who you been writing to?' he asked suspiciously.

'Just my grandmother. She sent me a present for my birthday, and I had to thank her.' Lucy hoped he wouldn't realize how long had passed since her birthday—but he seemed more bothered about something else.

'Where's she live, this grandmother?'

'In Exeter. It's too far away for me to see her. That's why I have to write.'

The Duke grunted, satisfied. 'That's all right, then,' he said. 'I don't want you going away, girl, not now. It's taken long enough to find you. Stolen away as a baby, you were, did I ever tell you that? And now I got you back.'

Lucy stared at him. Did he believe his own crazy stories? His china stare looked at the sky as if he had the innocence of a baby, but she felt more scared of him than she had ever done.

The Duke was in a mood of high good humour all day; selling his matches as usual and taking money while Lucy sang. He chatted to people and told his tall stories to anyone who would listen, and made no suggestion that they should go 'round the houses'. He spent a long time in the Three Tuns with some of his cronies, and seemed in no hurry to go home. By the time he drank the last of his beer and stood up, it was dark outside, and lamps were flaring above the stalls. 'That'll do, girl,' he said.

Lucy waited for him to put his hand on her shoulder. She had been wondering all day whether they would go back to the house or to somewhere else, and her question was soon answered. He set off in the usual direction, but when they reached the main road, the grip of his fingers tightened and he said, 'Turn left.'

This was new territory. They walked through street after unfamiliar street, then entered a maze of lanes and narrow alleys, some of them no more than slits between the high walls of warehouses. The Duke never faltered in his instructions to her, and after half an hour or so they came out to a broad dock further down the river, where an occasional light burned among the dark shapes of moored ships.

'Go right here,' the Duke said. 'Then up to Dockhead and round the top.'

Lucy wondered how he knew the way so exactly. Could he smell the difference of the air when the yeasty, spicy reek of the warehouses gave way to the river's cold breath of mud? Or maybe it was a remembered map of places he

113

used to know when he could still see. Plucking up her courage, she asked, 'Where are we going?'

For a few more paces, he did not answer. Then he said, 'That's no question for a granddaughter to ask. You disappoint me, girl.' He took her by the arm and pulled her close, and she could smell the beer on his breath. 'Families keeps their mouths shut. They don't ask, they wait to be told. Get me?'

Lucy was too scared to say anything, and she nodded, forgetting for a moment that he couldn't see her. His fingers dug painfully into her arm.

'I said, *Get me?*' He sounded threatening.

'Yes, I do,' she said quickly. 'I'm sorry.'

'You'll learn,' said the Duke. *As Daisy had learned*. And they walked on.

A clouded half-moon gave a dim light as they left the docks behind and skirted past mudflats and fishermen's huts. A cold wind blew from the estuary, full of the wet, rotten smell of the river. They passed small hovels made of scrap timber and an occasional upturned boat that was being used as a house, then came to a river inlet spanned by a narrow, wooden footbridge. Lucy helped the Duke up its steps. On the other side was a cluster of dilapidated wooden buildings that leaned towards each other like decaying trees, joined here and there by outflung galleries that spanned gaps as narrow and sinister as human rat-holes. The wet, dark walls seemed to grow from the water itself, either from the river or from a deep, almost empty ditch kept from the tidal flow of the Thames by a sluice-gate under the bridge.

Rookeries, Lucy thought, remembering a word she had heard used to describe the crowded slums. She saw now exactly what it meant. In this forest of ramshackle housing, the people were as close-packed as the rooks that built their nests in the elm trees, roosting and cawing and quarrelling among themselves, grabbing at whatever food could be found and spreading their ragged wings to batter against each other, lacking the air in which to fly.

She glanced back as she left the bridge with the Duke. The moon sailed free of its clouds and showed her the glint of water trickling over the top of the closed sluice-gate and down into the foul-smelling ditch. It was a moat, she thought. Once it was full of water, this place would be an island.

Then she knew where she was. *They call it Jacob's Island*, Tom had said. *Somewhere past the docks, down towards Rotherhithe*. Perhaps Finn would be there, waiting for her. Or Tom would already have rescued him, and they had gone away to somewhere safe.

'You want to know what this place is?' asked the Duke. He sounded triumphant.

'Yes, please,' Lucy said meekly. 'If you don't mind.'

'Wouldn't offer else, would I? This here's my castle. Didn't know that, did you?'

'No.' She hated it when he started on his fantasies. She was always scared he would realize that she didn't believe them.

'It's not the only one, not by a long chalk,' he went on. 'I got castles you couldn't dream of, a sight better than this. They don't call me the Duke for nothing. Left here.'

They turned into a narrow passage between the overhanging houses. 'Mind out,' Lucy said, steering the Duke away from the foul-smelling water and garbage that trickled down the middle of the alley. She wondered if they ever opened the sluice-gate and let the water in to run between the houses and wash all the rubbish away.

'This place here,' the Duke went on, 'I only keep it for charity. A free bed for them as falls on hard times. The Good Samaritan, that's what I am, girl. Done more for the

115

starving poor than any man alive. One of these days they'll have a statue to me in Trafalgar Square, never mind your Nelson. Waste of money that was, building a thing that high just to stick a little bloke like him on top.' Then he stopped without warning outside a closed door under an overhanging balcony, and banged on it with his fist, a pattern of slow and quick thumps that seemed like a signal. After a few minutes, there was a sound of bolts being drawn and a rusty key being turned, and Ada stood before them.

'You took your time,' she said.

'Couldn't come in daylight, could I,' said the Duke. 'Asking for trouble. All right, is it? Everything go good and proper?'

'Why shouldn't it?' said Ada.

The Duke chuckled. 'That's the stuff. Run things ourselves, eh? We'll be all right here. Home from home.'

Inside, the house was as dank and cold as a cellar. Lucy, with the Duke in front of her, followed the flickering light of Ada's candle along a dark corridor. Light beamed out as Ada opened a further door. There was a chatter of voices and a smell of boiling meat, and Lucy found herself in a steamy, crowded room. It was hardly different from the kitchen at the old house, except that it had no stove, only a fireplace where a pot hung over a crackling blaze of scrap timber. The same people sat round a table, drinking and laughing, and Daisy was perched on a man's knee, half-heartedly trying to stop him from pulling her low-cut blouse off her shoulder. Her bruised eye was still swollen and half-closed, and she was careful not to look in Lucy's direction.

Ada filled a mug with beer from the jug that stood on the table, and handed it to the Duke, and he raised it in celebration.

'I give you a toast,' he said to the assembled company. 'Here's to happy accident!'

There was a roar of laughter and shouts of, 'I'll drink to that!'

'What does he mean?' Lucy whispered to Slip, who was sitting on a crate nearby.

He looked up, grinning, and the dented blue scar shone livid in the firelight. 'Xavier Winterthorn,' he said. 'Fell out of his window, four o'clock this afternoon. Most unfortunate.' His face creased into fresh laughter.

'And is he—' But Lucy knew what she was going to hear.

'Dead,' said Slip. 'Stone, cold dead. They've taken him off to the city morgue.' He raised his tankard triumphantly. 'Cheers.'

10

That night, Lucy lay under a thin blanket on the kitchen floor of the damp, half-derelict house, too scared to sleep. The last of the firelight showed her the quick-moving shapes of rats as they scuffled and nibbled and sometimes ran across an outstretched hand or foot. She was as far away as she could get from the people who lay huddled like a litter of puppies for warmth, but their snoring and muttering disturbed her—and she could hear a thin whining, as if some other puppy had been left out in the cold.

Although she was very tired, Lucy's mind would not settle. It ran again and again over what had happened. Someone in the gang had killed Winterthorn, that was obvious. He had been their master, but he'd gone too far, like an over-confident lion tamer. Throwing the kitchen people out of the house had been a fatal step—they'd turned on him with all their half-hidden savagery.

And now what? Lucy knew she was playing a terribly dangerous game. She still needed to find out who had really killed Albert, because the police would never listen to her without some real evidence—but she hadn't meant to get as close to the gang as this. The Duke's crazy notion that she really was his granddaughter terrified her, and yet there was no way out of it. If they guessed the truth— Lucy shivered. A knife between the ribs, a cushion over the face, a body dumped in the Thames in the dark of the night.

The women who had brought the Duke home when

118

George had been ill would say there was no need to be afraid of dying. They believed there was another life in Heaven, better than this one—but Lucy could find no consolation in such an idea. She didn't want Heaven, she wanted the real world with all its imperfections. She loved rainwater lying between the cobbles and the good, strong smell of horses and the smoke of chestnuts roasting, and hot muffins bought from the man who carried a laden tray with a white cloth over it, ringing his bell through the streets. Angels in Heaven would have none of these things, just endless sky and the thin music of harps. Lucy knew she would yearn for mud and fog and seagulls and the real people who trundled barrels about and ate sausages, and most of all she would want Papa and Tom and Finn. And Miss Martin.

The teacher's voice came sharply to her mind. It sounded amused but firm.

*Lucy Bellman, will you please stop day-dreaming and **think**?*

Yes, Miss Martin, Lucy said silently. After the days of shouted orders from Ada, it was good to have a helpful instruction again. Obediently, she began to sort out her worries and concerns, trying to set them in order as she would for writing an essay. The one that came out on top of all the others was very simple. *I'm on my own. I need help.*

Perhaps Miss Martin could help her. Lucy thought of the note enclosed in the Latin primer. *I will be happy to hear from you at any time.* Would that still be true? Young ladies who went to Miss Martin's Academy did not get themselves mixed up with people like Slip and the Duke and Ada. She might be shocked.

I can't help that, Lucy thought. *I must see her.* But it would mean escaping from this place and finding her way back through the maze of streets to the school. And Lucy wouldn't be able to talk to her teacher in front of the other girls, so she'd have to wait until they'd all gone home. No, it was impossible. She could never get away on her own for such a long time. She was constantly with the Duke or working in the house. He and Ada didn't let her out of their sight.

They might send me on an errand, she thought. Her mind began to fill with a half-dream of walking through the streets towards Miss Martin, free from all this dreadfulness. The whining dog was quiet now. Lucy turned on her side, and at last she slept.

Next morning, the room smelt stuffy and foul. Ada came in with a couple of loaves and a gallon jug of ale and said, 'Breakfast.'

Lucy was still huddled in her blanket, feeling chilled and stiff.

'What's the matter with you?' Ada demanded.

'There was a dog whining or something. I couldn't sleep.' She wasn't sure now what the noise had been. It had gone on through her dreams.

'Dog?' said Ada.

'Yes. It was downstairs somewhere. Or outside, perhaps.'

'You don't want to worry about that,' said Ada. 'It's just a stray. Here, cut these loaves up.'

And Lucy did as she was told.

She expected to go out with the Duke as usual, but when the blind man got to his feet Ada stood up as well.

'You're stopping here,' she said to Lucy. 'Get the place cleared up. You'll find water out the back—there's a bucket. And if anyone comes to the door, don't answer.'

'I won't,' Lucy promised.

She smiled to herself. It was easy to look cheerful and

120

willing, because to be left alone in the house was exactly what she wanted. She would slip out as soon as they'd gone, and with any luck she could be at Miss Martin's school within an hour. She might even catch her teacher for a quick word at the morning break and be back before she was missed.

Ada was putting on a rusty old black bonnet that hid most of her face. She tied its greasy ribbons then draped a moth-eaten shawl round her shoulders and took the Duke's arm. Together, they looked a harmless, shabby couple, no different from hundreds of others.

Lucy followed the pair of them to the front door. Everyone else had already gone out.

'Peel some potatoes for supper,' Ada instructed. 'And get the fire lit for this evening. There's plenty of scrap wood lying about. You'll find an axe by the fireplace.'

'Yes, all right.' There would be time to do all that when she came back from Miss Martin's.

Ada and the Duke went out—but when the heavy door closed behind them, Lucy heard the grind and click of a key being turned in the lock. She stood, frozen with dismay, then flung herself at the handle, turning it desperately. The door would not budge. She was a prisoner.

She ran from room to empty room, looking for a way out. She hauled open shutters that creaked and spilled rust, letting in the river's light to ripple across stained walls and flaking ceilings, but every window was barred with rough bits of wood nailed across what was left of their glass. A door that probably led to the cellar was locked. With pounding heart, she scrambled up the rickety staircase to the first floor and looked into rooms empty of furniture but for an occasional orange box or basket and a scatter of clothes and blankets. No way out here—every door that looked as if it might lead through to another part of the building was barred. Lucy ran up the second flight of stairs, and a rattle of wings startled her as pigeons flew out through gaps in the roof. Bird droppings littered the rotten floors in a warren of attics and the place smelt foul, but a crack of bright daylight came from the edge of a door that stood slightly ajar. Lucy flung it open—and found herself standing at the edge of the sky.

Dizzy with the shock of it, she clung to the door jamb as if one more step would launch her into emptiness. For a moment she hardly saw the projecting roof above her head or the narrow balcony in front of her, edged by a wooden rail with several bars missing. Then, very cautiously, she tried her weight on the split and rotten boards. They felt solid enough, so she stepped forward, put her hands on the rail's edge and looked down. A long way below, the sluggish river lapped along the walls of the house and against the barrier of the sluice-gate that kept the water from the ditch. She could see the bridge she had crossed with the Duke last night and the buildings that hid the streets she had come through, but they could have been as far away as the moon.

A bucket stood at her feet, tied to the rail by a long, frayed bit of rope. *You'll find water out the back*, Ada had said. Lucy fingered the rope, wondering for a crazy moment if it would bear her weight, but the idea died almost before it had entered her mind. She would fall and drown. She stared across the river at the distant bank. There were boats hauled up on the mud or leaning sideways on the grass between a few tarred huts further up, but they were much too far away to be of any use.

Other people were using boats for whatever purposes they chose. A big merchantman was making its way up to the docks, and barges with brown sprit-sails rode low in the water because of the heavy loads they carried. In between them, small boats were being rowed about in the same busy way that market traders trundled their barrows

122

around the cobbled streets. They were all free to go about their normal business. Lucy waved at them frantically for a few minutes, and once an arm waved back from behind a half-furled sail, but it was no more than a casual greeting. Nobody realized that she needed help.

Tears of rage and disappointment filled Lucy's eyes, but she blinked them away angrily. There was no use in crying. She stooped for the bucket and let it down into the water. Since there was no escape from this place, she might as well do what she could to make it less unpleasant—and to keep Ada happy.

The rest of the day dragged by. Lucy scrubbed and swept, lit the fire and peeled the potatoes and, as the afternoon darkened, Ada and the Duke came back, saying nothing to Lucy about where they had been. Their friends straggled in and a pot of tripe and onions was cooked over the fire, together with the potatoes. Beer was drunk and noisy songs were sung, and then came another uncomfortable night of half dream and half waking, haunted by the whining dog.

'Got a job for you tonight,' the Duke said to her the next morning.

'What is it?' Lucy knew she sounded rude, but she was too tired to care.

'You'll be coming out with Slip and me.'

'Where to?'

'Them as asks no questions isn't told no lies,' said the Duke, but his hand found her hair and ruffled it. 'You're a good girl. My little granddaughter.'

And that was all she could get out of him.

When they had gone out, locking the door behind them, Lucy ran upstairs like a caged animal, to stare out at the freedom that was so cruelly out of reach. Without meaning to, she found herself making a noise very much like the whining dog, crying aloud to the sky and the river in a wild complaint that had no words.

Nobody answered, of course. There was no one out there, only the gulls that wheeled against the grey clouds. She turned and went back into the house.

Through the long hours of another day, Lucy kept herself busy, but as the daylight began to fade, she went out on the balcony again and stared across the river. It was pink-flushed with sunset now and very beautiful, even though it kept her a prisoner. In despair, she said aloud, 'I'll never get away.'

And a voice answered from somewhere quite close above her, 'Yes, you will.'

I'm going mad, thought Lucy. *People do go mad, don't they, when things get to be too awful.* Everything round her seemed real and normal—the wood beneath her feet, the bucket, the sunset—but that could be part of it. Dreams always seemed real when they were happening and maybe madness was the same. Being mad, you wouldn't know if it was normal or not.

In the next moment, there was a loud scraping noise above her as if some enormous bird had landed on the overhanging roof. Then a boot appeared from over the edge, followed by a skinny ankle sticking out of a brown trouser-leg. The boot waved as if groping for a foothold— and Lucy suddenly knew whose it was.

'*Tom!*' She steered his foot to the railing, and he jumped down to stand beside her. 'Oh, Tom, you're an angel!' He really did seem like an angel, come from Heaven when she most needed him.

'Don't be daft,' said Tom.

'But it's like magic! Where have you come from?'

'Over the roof. There's a way up from next door, you get on the window sill, then the balcony.'

'But how did you know I was here?' Lucy asked.

'I saw you yesterday. I was out in a boat with Starkey. I couldn't get here before—I'm working for him, scraping hulls and painting.'

'Who's Starkey?'

'A fisherman. He found me sleeping under one of his boats—he's a good sort. Lucy, what are you doing here? Did they bring you from the other house?'

'Yes. Mr Winterthorn's dead.'

'I know,' said Tom. 'I met Daisy—she told me. And Finn's downstairs in the cellar,' he rushed on. 'Slip and the Duke made him climb through a window when he was out with them one night, and he fell and gashed his knee. It's his bad leg, and it went septic and he couldn't walk at all, so they shut him up there. He's had a fever; I thought he was going to die.'

'Tom, I've heard him!' Lucy thumped her forehead with her hand. *The whining in the night.* 'Why didn't I realize? They said it was a dog. I found a door to the cellar from the house, but it's locked.'

Tom nodded. 'That's what Daisy said. And there's a grating in the lane. You can see down through the bars, but it's fixed, you can't get in that way. I've been putting bits of bread in for Finn, and talking to him. But I can't get him out.'

Lucy stared at him, aghast. 'What are we going to do?'

'I don't know,' said Tom. He looked older than when she last saw him, although it was less than a week ago. In the moment of silence that followed, her ideas of what was most important shifted. Little Finn had to be rescued before anything else.

'We've got to get help,' she said. 'I'll find a way out of here somehow, and go and ask my teacher. Slip and the

Duke are taking me out somewhere tonight, I could do it then. I'll just run.'

'That won't work,' Tom told her. 'They'd probably catch you. And even if you get away, it won't do any good. They'll expect you to tell the police, so they'll leave the house and go somewhere else before anyone comes looking for them, and take Finn with them. Then I won't know where he is. They might even kill him. And you'll never find out who murdered Albert.'

He was right. And it was dangerous, too. If the Duke caught her trying to make a break for it—Lucy shuddered at the thought. 'Then *you'll* have to get help,' she said. 'Ask Miss Martin—you know where the school is, don't you? The one I used to go to. I wish I could tell her myself,' she added, 'but you're right—I'll have to stay here.'

'You'd never get over the roofs anyway, not with skirts and everything,' Tom said practically.

Lucy made a face. 'I wish I hadn't been born a girl. It's not fair.'

'Oh, I don't know,' said Tom. 'I like you the way you are.'

For the first time in days, Lucy smiled. Somehow, his words had brought her a rush of happiness.

'I must go,' Tom went on. 'I'll find your Miss Martin.' Then he looked at her, frowning. 'Be careful tonight. They probably want you along instead of Finn, but mind what you say. Don't let them know what you really think.'

'I won't,' Lucy promised. She was well used to being careful by now.

Tom climbed onto the railing then heaved himself up to the overhanging roof.

'I'll see you tomorrow,' he said. 'Good luck.'

'You, too,' said Lucy. And she heard the scrape and slither of his boots on the tiles as he went clambering away.

126

* * *

That night, the Duke stood up and put his coat on, then said, 'Where's that girl? Time we were going.' Obediently, Lucy reached for her shawl, but Ada thrust a bundle of clothing into her arms and said, 'Wear these. You can change upstairs.'

By the light of a candle that flickered in the draught, Lucy found she had been given a pair of moleskin trousers, stained and shabby, together with a flannel shirt, a waistcoat, and a rough jacket. So tonight she was to be a boy. Tom's guess must have been right—she was a replacement for Finn.

'Hurry up!' Ada yelled from downstairs, and Lucy shouted back, 'Coming!'

Hastily, she took off her own things and climbed into the unfamiliar garments. She wished she did not have to go on this adventure—but she knew she must. Her hands felt cold and clammy as she walked downstairs in the rough clothes, and her heart was thumping fast, but she held her head up boldly. It was important to look brave and excited, as a real granddaughter of the Duke would.

There was a gale of laughter from the people in the room as Lucy came in wearing her boy's clothes, but she ignored it. With both hands, she smoothed her hair back and said to Ada, 'I need a hat or something.'

Ada leaned forward and grabbed a cap from the head of a big, carroty-haired lad who sat chewing at a mutton chop by the fire. She cuffed him as he made a snatch at it and said, 'You'll get it back.' Then she tossed the cap to Lucy. It was stained and greasy and far too large, but Lucy pulled it on and tucked all the escaping strands of her hair into it.

'That's better,' said Ada.

'Where are we going?' asked Lucy.

127

'You'll see,' said the Duke. He was on his feet, looking heavy-shouldered and impatient, with Slip beside him.

'Keep quiet, that's the main thing,' Ada said in Lucy's ear. 'And do exactly what they tell you.'

Lucy nodded, dry-mouthed. And then she followed the two men out.

The Duke walked with more confidence than he usually did, hardly needing to put his hand on Lucy's shoulder. The night was an extension of his private darkness, she thought. He didn't find it mysterious or frightening, because he was used to it. She almost felt sorry for him, belonging in a world where there was no light or colour, but just then he gave her a hard push and said, 'Don't dawdle about, we haven't got all night.'

'Sorry.' She hadn't thought she was dawdling.

They had left the streets behind now, and were walking across rough land where the dark shapes of cattle mingled their warm scent with the smells of dung and trodden grass. Lucy stumbled sometimes, unused to the muddy, rutted surface. Her mind went back to Penge Common and the last carefree walk she had taken with her father to her grandparents' house, before all this started. What a happy dream it had all been—and at the time, she hadn't known it was a dream. She had found things to grumble at, and disliked Ada simply because she was sometimes rude and bossy. *If I ever go back to that*, she thought, *I will be grateful for ever*. But the idea of return was a dream, too. The reality was now, stumbling along in the dark, dressed in strange clothes, with two men who were up to no good.

The moon came out from behind ragged clouds, showing up the roofs and chimneys of some big houses. They could have been the ones she and the Duke had visited, Lucy thought uneasily. Certainly the Duke seemed to know where he was, for he turned his face to her and put a warning finger to his lips. 'We're going in here,' he said quietly.

Lucy nodded, then remembered quickly that he could not see her. 'All right,' she said, dry-mouthed.

'Come on, then,' said Slip. 'Over the railing.'

The Duke already had his hand on an iron rail that ran between shrubs and trees at the edge of a large garden, and he grabbed Lucy's arm and pushed her towards it. For a moment she stooped as if to gather up her skirts, then realized there was no need—in her trousers, she was free of all that clinging fabric. Like a little girl in short frocks again, she put one foot on the lower rail and swung the other one over. She jumped down into the wet grass and whispered, 'Where now?'

'Back of the house,' the Duke muttered. 'Kitchen.'

They made their way towards it. *I'm a trusted member of the family*, Lucy reminded herself. *I must make sure they go on trusting me.*

They trod quietly across the lawn and then over a paved yard with a stable block on one side, joined to the back of the house by a wall with an arch in it. Slip was ahead of them, moving towards the back door, where he waited. The Duke stopped at a narrow window near the door. It was tightly closed, but he ran his hands over the frame of it then took a heavy clasp-knife from his pocket and pushed the blade into the wood. There was a click, and he grunted with satisfaction, putting the knife back in his pocket. Slip pulled the window open. It was no more than a narrow fanlight hinged at the top, and it looked impossibly small.

The Duke turned to Lucy. 'In you go,' he said.

It was the command she had dreaded. She looked at the narrow space in horror, certain she couldn't get through it. 'I can't!' she breathed.

Slip grabbed her. 'Lift her feet up,' he muttered to the

129

Duke, and in the next minute she was being pushed roughly through the tight opening.

'Turn sideways,' hissed the Duke. 'Get your arms up over your head.'

Something hard was scraping painfully along her chest, and the side of her face caught against the narrow frame, knocking off the greasy cap—but she was through. She expected to put a foot to the floor, but she couldn't—she was on the same level as the window's edge.

'It's a table,' Lucy gasped. She sensed that there were objects near to her in the darkness, and was terrified that she might be going to knock something over—a jug, a bread-crock, a pan of milk.

The Duke put his head through the window. 'If you wake the household, you're on your own,' he whispered fiercely. 'So shut up. Go round to the back door and unbolt it.'

Very carefully, Lucy wriggled backwards off the table, feeling for the floor. She stood upright, trembling with fear and trying to make out where she was. The small room smelt of soap and stale water, and she guessed it was a scullery or a wash-house. As her eyes got used to the darkness, she saw a door to her left, and crept towards it. The latch gave a slight click as she lifted it, and she froze. Silence hummed in her ears. She crept forward again, into a narrow passage. Feeling her way along the wall, she found the door and patted down the side of it until her fingers met the iron bulk of a large key. Holding her breath, she turned it slowly until the lock clicked over. Her hands were shaking. *Unbolt it*, the Duke had said. Was there a bolt as well? She groped again, and found it, just below the lock. This was harder, an obstinate hulk of a thing that scraped loudly in its housing as she tried to shift it. Gritting her teeth, she worked it up and down to loosen it, and at last managed to move it along. Then she eased the latch up and pulled the door open, and Slip slid in beside her, followed by the Duke.

Lucy waited to guide the blind man, even though a part of her mind urged her to run through the open door and away—but he pushed past her with no apparent need for her help, moving along the passage as if he knew the house well. Lucy followed him.

Slip had opened the door to a room, and the two men went in. Lucy stood behind the Duke and stared. The glow of an almost dead fire in the grate gleamed in the curtained warmth and picked out points of brightness from the silverware and glass ranged in glazed cupboards and on a huge sideboard. Slip hauled a sack from an inside pocket of his coat and the Duke, with deft certainty, began to put dishes and plates into it. And then Lucy knew the truth. The Duke's movements were too quick and sure for those of a blind man. He could see.

Lucy gasped. Her hand was over her mouth, but the Duke heard her. He turned his head, and she saw the blank whiteness of his artificial eye—but saw too the glint of mad intelligence in the real one, usually half shut and seeming sightless. He smiled. Then he picked up a bottle that stood on the sideboard among others, and uncorked it. Still looking at her in a kind of triumph, he took a long, deliberate swig. The fire's dim light showed his powerful, meaty hands, and Lucy felt sick with appalled understanding. Those hands probably killed Albert.

The Duke beckoned her towards him. 'You want some?' he whispered, offering her the bottle. 'My little granddaughter?'

Lucy shook her head and backed away, too scared now to worry about whether he trusted her—and his face changed. He grabbed her by the arm. 'Don't you let me down, girl,' he whispered, his brandy-smelling breath close in her face. 'You love your old grandfather, don't you. Your grandpa what can see.' He pushed the bottle into one of the deep pockets of his coat, and put his hands on her shoulders. Then he moved them almost gently up to her neck, thumbs close on each side of her windpipe. His caressing voice held an edge that was like a honed knife. 'Say you love him, darling. Say you love Grandpa.'

Panic swept over Lucy, and she had no thought except to get away before he killed her. She kicked out wildly at his shins and he grunted and slapped her hard across the face. Lucy screamed and he slapped her again.

Twisting and turning in the Duke's grasp, Lucy saw Slip bolt out of the room. A flicker of candle-light came from the passage, and the Duke cursed. He flung Lucy to the floor and aimed a kick at her, then he ran as well. There was shouting, and the light went out. Lucy heard a scuffle at the back door, a yell and a thump and running footsteps. Then there was silence.

Someone was coming back into the room. Lucy was struggling to sit up as a large shape filled the doorway. *They've come back for me*, she thought. And she screamed and went on screaming.

'Stop that noise, you silly girl.'

It wasn't Slip or the Duke—the person who hauled Lucy to her feet was a fat woman in a flannel nightgown. She smelt of sweat and sleep and her hair was in curling papers, and in her free hand she held a poker. A new and steadier light bloomed outside as someone started down the stairs.

'There,' said the woman, 'you've gone and woken the master.'

An elderly man came into the room with a lamp in one hand and a pistol in the other. He set the lamp on the sideboard without hurry and looked with interest at the abandoned sack on the floor and at Lucy.

132

'Well, Bess,' he said to the woman, 'I see you have caught a burglar.' His feet were in scuffed leather slippers and he wore a quilted black smoking jacket over his nightshirt.

'Yes, sir,' said the woman. 'The other two made off, but I gave one of them a clout over the head.'

'I'm not a burglar,' said Lucy.

'No?' the man queried. 'Then what are you, pray, and why are you in my house?'

It was a fair question. 'I'm a burglar's assistant,' Lucy admitted. She still felt breathless. Her face hurt and she could taste blood from a cut lip, and her hair, loosened when the cap had fallen off, was all over the place. 'I'm very sorry. I didn't want to be, but I got sort of . . . caught.' This was a disaster. She had done exactly what Tom had warned her not to do, and she daren't think what would happen now.

The tassel of the man's nightcap hung over one of his bushy eyebrows and made him look faintly comic, but his voice was crisp. 'Caught by whom?' he enquired. 'And why are you dressed up in male attire?'

'Slip and the Duke said I had to. I thought the Duke was blind, but he isn't. I've been shut up in this house, you see. And Ada said—'

The man sighed and put his gun down beside the lamp. 'Bess,' he said, 'could you make some tea?'

'Yes, sir. And shall I wake Walter?'

'Do that. But tell him he needn't get up unless I ring the bell.'

The fat woman gave a little curtsy and went off along the passage.

'You, my dear, had better sit down,' said the man.

The explanations took a long time, and Lucy began to feel

133

more and more agitated. Slip and the Duke would be back at the house any minute now, and once the gang knew what had happened, they would desert the place like rats. She had let Tom down. He'd never find Finn. And she would never be able to prove her father's innocence.

'Your father is in prison, you say. What is his name?' The questions were continuing, patient and unhurried.

'Jeremy Bellman.'

'Ah, yes. My colleague is dealing with the case. I am myself in the legal profession, I should explain. George Cavendish. Forgive me, I should have introduced myself earlier.'

Lucy was getting desperate. She must find out what was happening at the house, dangerous or not. 'Mr Cavendish,' she said, 'you've been very kind, but I really ought to go now.'

He shook his head. 'You have no suitable place to go to, and I would be failing in my duty if I allowed a young lady to leave here at this time of night, on her own. Bess can make up a bed for you, and I'll deal with the rest of this business in the morning.'

'But I *can't*!' Lucy almost shouted. 'Don't you see, once the Duke gets back there, he'll tell them what's happened. They won't just wait for the police to come, they'll leave the house. And Tom's little brother is there like I told you, and if he's too ill to move they'll just leave him to die, or they might even kill him. Oh, *please*! I've *got* to go!'

Cavendish looked at her thoughtfully, pulling at his lip. Then, without a further word, he got up and went out. From the yard, Lucy heard the loud ringing of the stable bell.

11

Lucy clung tightly to Mr Cavendish as she sat behind him on the black horse, riding astride in her moleskin trousers. The stableman rode beside them as they galloped through the night, and the sack across his saddle bow clinked rhythmically. 'Bring some tools, Walter,' Cavendish had told him. 'Heavy ones. And sharp.' And the man had gone off without so much as the raising of an eyebrow to do his master's bidding.

The horses slackened pace as they entered a cobbled lane near the river, and Cavendish turned his head to ask, 'Which way now?'

'This comes out by a bridge,' Lucy told him. 'It goes over the ditch, by the sluice-gate. The house is on the other side.'

The clattering hooves were loud in the narrow space between the house-walls, then quietened suddenly as they came out into the open.

It looked different. The water seemed closer now, and it was making a greedy, rushing sound, very different from the slack rippling Lucy had become used to. As they came closer, she saw that a flood was pouring into the ditch, filling it so fast that it already almost washed the underside of the footbridge.

'They've let the river in!' she cried. 'The gate's open!' The moon's pale glow shone from behind the black group of ramshackle houses and reflected from water that was fast encircling them. 'Oh, quickly!'

'I'm not taking the horses over that bridge,' said Cavendish. 'It might collapse. Off you get.'

Walter had already dismounted, and came to help Lucy down. He tied the horses to the rail and asked, 'You'll want the tools, sir?'

'Probably,' said Cavendish. He had his pistol in his hand.

Lucy followed him across the bridge, with Walter behind her. She didn't want to look down at the rushing brown water. The tide was rising, and Finn was probably still shut in the cellar. She gave a little sob of fear, and Cavendish glanced back at her.

'Tom's brother,' she blurted. 'If the water goes in the cellar, he'll drown.'

Walter said, 'They've chained the gate open. Blooming great padlock, look. And an iron bar.'

'Well, free it, man,' said Cavendish impatiently. 'You've brought the tools, use them. Lucy, show me the house.'

Lucy ran after him. For a crazy moment, she expected him to put his hand on her shoulder like the Duke, but this was different. 'It's here,' she said.

Cavendish tried the door but it was locked, as Lucy expected. He hammered on it with the butt of his pistol and, receiving no answer, stood back and stared up at the dark windows with their dirty, broken panes. 'If there's anyone there, open up!' he shouted.

Several people had come out of other houses, ragged and suspicious.

'What's all the row about?'

'Who is he?'

'What's he want?'

Cavendish turned to face them. 'Have any of you seen a man known as the Duke?'

Heads were shaken, and mouths tightened. Even by

136

the thin light of the moon, Lucy caught the glances that were exchanged. A woman shouted, 'Why don't you shove off and leave us alone? We ain't done nothing.'

I must see about Finn, Lucy thought. She slipped away, leaving Cavendish to argue with the crowd. The narrow lane Tom had spoken of sloped down by the side of the house, and after only a few yards she found the grating at her feet, close to the wall. A crawling fringe of scummy water was creeping towards it between the cobbles, washing closer with every moment that passed. She knelt down and stared into the darkness under the bars.

'Finn!' she called. 'Are you there?'

She thought she caught a faint sound—a creak as if someone moved on a rickety bed. 'Finn!' she shouted louder. '*Finn!* It's me, Lucy. Can you hear me?'

Something was moving beneath her in the darkness, a white shape. Finn's face was just below the grating, staring up at her. 'Lucy! Is it really you?'

'Yes. I've come to get you out.'

The plan that had flashed into her mind made her feel sick with fear, but it was the only way. *I've got to do it*, she thought. *Got to.*

'I prayed someone would come,' Finn said.

He put his hand up between the bars, and Lucy gripped it tightly. 'I'm going to find a way in,' she promised him. 'Tom told me how. Then I'll break the cellar door down. There's an axe in the kitchen.'

The rising flood was making the knees of her trousers wet as she knelt there, and water was already trickling into the cellar, dripping on Finn's upturned face. Lucy gave the little boy's hand a last squeeze and said, 'I'll be as quick as I can.' She stood up and saw his fingers disappear from the grating, then ran round to the front of the house.

To her relief, Cavendish and the crowd had moved

down to the bridge and the sluice-gate, where Walter was still hammering. A woman with a baby in her arms looked at her with idle curiosity then turned and went into a dark doorway, and Lucy was alone in the street.

What had Tom said? Something about the window sill of the house next door. The thought of the danger ahead lay like a cold stone of dread in her stomach. *I can't. I just can't.* But she knew she would have to, and quickly, before Cavendish realized what she meant to do and prevented it.

Lucy ducked into the darkness under the overhanging balcony and ran her palms across the walls and the shuttered window. She could find no hand-hold. She turned and looked up at the dark bulk of the balcony against the sky, and the cloudy moon showed her a diagonal support running from the wall to the underside of the balcony. That must be what Tom had meant. She climbed onto the window sill, digging her fingers into gaps in the closed and rotten shutters to support herself, then reached for the slanting bar and hauled herself up to a hole in the boards of the balcony. She got her elbows through and scrambled onto the cracked planks of its floor, then got to her feet. *Now what?*

Staring up, she saw that the roof above her was just within reach. She climbed onto the balcony rail and crouched there for a moment, getting her balance, then cautiously stood up and put her hands on the roof's edge. There was nothing to get hold of. Then her exploring hand found a gap where a tile was missing, and she hooked her fingers into it to heave herself up. In the next minute, she was crawling over the tiles.

The worst bit lay ahead. Lucy remembered how Tom's foot had waved blindly as it tried to find the rail of the narrow balcony at the back of the house, set back as it was under the overhang of the roof. If he had missed it, he'd have fallen down the sheer drop into the river. And she wasn't as tall as Tom, so it would be harder to reach the rail. She went on working her way up the slope of the crumbling tiles, and felt more dizzy and sick with every inch she gained.

She reached the ridge and got one knee across, then sat astride it for a moment, trying to get a few deeper breaths into her panting lungs. But there was no time to lose. She turned herself round so as to start the downward slope feet first. Her elbows were still over the ridge, holding her weight, but she had to let go.

Lucy knew now why Tom's boots had slithered and scraped—it was only an occasional hole in the roof that gave her anything to hang on to. Several times she slid dreadfully fast, grating the skin off her fingers and sick with the terror of falling over the edge. She heard Cavendish shout from the street, 'Lucy! Where are you?'

Lucy couldn't have shouted back, even if she'd wanted to. Her breath was fluttering with fright and she clung desperately to a bit of rotten joist where several tiles had caved in. Her feet were scrabbling for a grip, and she felt the timbers cracking underneath her. She grabbed frantically for a firmer hold, but the roof was giving way, she was falling—

The floor hit Lucy so hard all over that it knocked the breath out of her. Choking dust filled her nose and mouth. For a few moments she lay still, half stunned and not sure that the boards below her might not give way as well. She coughed, then rolled over and sat up. Her left wrist hurt badly and she nursed it for a moment in her other hand, biting her lip. But at least she wasn't in the water. The moon shining through the hole in the roof showed her the walls of a small room, and she saw it was one of the attic ones on the top floor, near the balcony. She struggled to her feet—and then heard something that

139

made her freeze with horror. Heavy footsteps were coming up the stairs.

Lucy flattened herself against the wall. The footsteps came to a halt outside. Then the door slowly opened, and the moonlight was blocked out by a dark figure.

'There you are,' said the Duke. 'Come home after all. My little girl.' He seemed to be swaying slightly as he moved towards her.

'No!' Lucy could manage no more than a dry whisper. He reached out and took her by the arm, causing a stab of pain in her injured wrist.

'I'm disappointed in you, girl,' he said. 'You and me, we could have shown 'em a thing or two. We're the same sort, I knew that right away. First time I saw you, I thought, there's the right girl for my granddaughter. A girl who knows what's right and proper, not like the others.' The smell of Cavendish's brandy came from him in waves, mixed with the usual reek of his dirty clothes and unwashed body, and Lucy realized that he was very drunk. She wondered if she could make a dive for the gap between him and the door, but she dared not even glance at it in case he saw her intention. He was still holding her arm.

'My castles.' The white stare of his unseeing eye glittered in the moonlight, though she knew the other one was watching her. 'Nothing left now. All rotten. Rotten wood, rotten people. Clean 'em up, girl, that's the only way. Get rid of it all, start again. I dealt with Slip.' He gave a dry chuckle. 'Ada ran off, but I'll catch up with her. And now there's you.' He shifted his grasp to Lucy's shoulder. 'I'm sorry about you, girl. I thought you were different.'

His grip tightened as he pulled her towards him, and Lucy gave a breathless scream.

'Ain't no use you shouting,' said the Duke. 'There's

nobody here can help you. All gone, all rotten. You, too.'
He was turning her round, forcing her out of the door
ahead of him—and Lucy suddenly knew what he was
going to do. The balcony . . . the river.

'Please!' she gasped. 'Oh, no, please!'

The Duke laughed. He opened the door to the balcony
and thrust her out onto the wooden boards, backing her
against the rail. 'That's nice,' he said. 'I like it when they
start asking favours. Bit late for that, girl.'

Lucy screamed. She went on screaming, ducking her
head away and struggling to free herself from his grip
despite the agonizing pain in her wrist. He grabbed at her
throat, fingers digging in behind her ear, and brought his
other hand up to cover her mouth. She bit him, hard.

'You little—'

The Duke lashed out at her, but Lucy ducked, then
kicked his shin. He staggered and half lost his balance—
and his foot went into the bucket that was tethered to the
rail by its length of rope. Flailing drunkenly, he stooped to
try and pull it off, but tipped sideways and lurched against
the wooden railing. It splintered under his weight, and
for an instant his arms cut across the moon like a
windmill's circling sails. Then he fell outwards, and the
snaking rope followed him until it snapped.

Lucy heard the heavy splash from far below her as she
panted for breath, clutching her injured wrist to her chest.
Then she turned and blundered into the house. Finn, she
must get to Finn.

On the first floor landing she tripped over something
bulky and soft, and almost fell. The soft thing groaned and
moved a little. 'Help me,' it said—and Lucy realized what
she was looking at.

'Daisy!' She crouched beside the girl in the darkness
and felt how cold she was. The floor round her seemed to
be wet and sticky.

'Knife.' Daisy's voice was a thin whisper. 'He had a knife.'

'The Duke?' But Lucy could not wait for a reply. 'I'll come back in just a moment, promise.' She groped her way down the next flight of stairs and into the kitchen, grabbed the axe from beside the fireplace and attacked the cellar door, one-handed because of her damaged wrist. People were hammering at the front door and Cavendish was shouting, 'Lucy, are you in there?' He sounded frantic.

'Open up!' It was a different man shouting—an official-sounding voice.

'I can't,' Lucy yelled, 'it's locked from outside. I've got to get into the cellar.'

Finn was screaming. 'Lucy, it's all water in here! It's over my knees!'

'Don't worry, I'm coming.' Lucy was almost sobbing with the one-handed effort. She threw her weight against the door, but it felt as solid as ever. Water was trickling from under it, creeping across the floor.

She hacked again. Her shoulder and arm felt on fire, and her strength was failing. A splintering crash came from the front of the house, then a crunching of quick footsteps towards her. The axe was grabbed from her hand. 'Mind out.'

'*Tom!*'

He didn't stop to answer. Chips flew as he attacked the wood savagely, and after a few moments he stood back and kicked hard at the lock. The door burst open.

Water gushed over their feet. Finn was sobbing in the darkness.

Tom plunged down the cellar steps, knee-deep then waist-deep. A light wavered behind Lucy and grew stronger, and the official voice asked, 'What's going on here?'

Lucy turned and was dazzled by the beam of a bull's-eye

142

lantern. The man directed it into the cellar instead, and she glimpsed his heavy police cape and helmet. A lot of other people had come in as well, together with Cavendish and Walter, who held a large hammer.

Tom waded up out of the cellar, carrying Finn in his arms. Water was pouring from their clothes. 'Just in time,' he said to Lucy. 'Thanks to you. And Miss Martin.'

'Miss Martin? But—'

'She's outside,' said Tom. 'We got a cab and came straight here. With the policeman.'

'I'm not outside.' Miss Martin emerged from the crowd, sounding as crisp as ever. 'I climbed in through the window like everyone else, since Walter and the policeman had so helpfully broken it.' She came towards them, holding her skirts clear of the wet floor. 'Lucy, my dear, are you all right?'

'Yes,' said Lucy faintly though her wrist throbbed badly and she ached all over. In the dark house, with the policeman's lantern glinting across the pool of water that dripped from Tom and Finn, she felt suddenly as if she was dreaming. She shook herself awake—there was something urgent to be done.

'Please, Miss Martin, come and see Daisy—she's upstairs. She's hurt.'

The policeman shone his lantern on Lucy and asked, 'Who is Daisy?'

'She used to work for them, but—'

Her words were interrupted by a gasp from Miss Martin as she saw Lucy's face in the beam of light. 'Oh, my dear! What have you done?'

'Nothing. I hurt my wrist, but—'

'You're covered with blood!'

Lucy glanced at her hands and saw the red staining on them, and knew what the wetness surrounding Daisy had been.

He had a knife.

'She's been stabbed! Oh, quickly!'

Lucy ran to the stairs. Miss Martin was behind her, followed by the excited crowd.

'Stand back, please!' the policeman ordered.

The lantern beam showed Daisy lying very still in the pool of blood. Miss Martin stooped for the girl's wrist, feeling the pulse. 'She's still alive,' she murmured.

The policeman crouched as well. 'Stab wound in the chest,' he said. He looked up and added, 'Somebody get a doctor, quickly.'

'Who's going to pay him?' a woman in the crowd demanded, and Cavendish said, 'I will. For God's sake, hurry.'

The woman and several of her friends went out.

Blood was still welling from the deep wound just above the low neck of Daisy's dress. Her lips moved as if she was trying to say something and Lucy bent close, kneeling beside her.

'Daisy, what is it?'

'The Duke—'

'What about him?' asked the policeman, pencil poised above his notebook.

'He's . . . killing everyone. Mad.' Her voice was faint. 'Be careful.'

'It's all right,' Lucy told her. 'He fell in the river.' She was going to add, 'I expect he's dead,' but she could not quite believe it. She had a vision of the Duke coming back, like a dripping, powerful ghost, and she couldn't speak the words.

A buzz of excitement had run through the crowd.

'In the river?'

'What happened?'

'The Duke, drowned?'

Cavendish cut across the babble of voices. 'Walter,

you'd better ride back to the house and tell Bess to get some beds made up. Then come back with the carriage.'

'I've a cab waiting by the bridge,' said Miss Martin. 'Tom and the little boy can come back with me if you prefer. And Lucy, too.'

'A kind offer, madam,' Cavendish said, 'but I have promised Miss Bellman my legal services, and I shall need to talk to her in some detail.'

Lucy would have liked nothing better than to go away from here with Tom and Finn and her beloved teacher—but she saw that Mr Cavendish was offering her a chance she could never have dreamed of, to sort this whole affair out and free her father. She smiled at him, and was going to thank him when a wave of giddiness rose from nowhere, and she was overwhelmed by the pain in her wrist and the sick knowledge that her legs were going to give way.

She was lying on the floor, wrapped in blankets. Tom was chopping wood with the axe, piling the pieces on a fire that was starting to blaze in the grate, and a man in shirt sleeves and a black waistcoat was bending over Lucy, feeling her wrist carefully.

'This is broken,' he said to someone behind him. 'And she's covered in bruises.' His fingers touched her face gently. 'Cut lip, abrasion to the cheek. A bad case of assault, I'd say.'

Lucy struggled to understand what had happened. Someone must have carried her downstairs. They had been standing beside Daisy. Fear swept over her.

'Daisy. Is she—' The question was too hard to ask.

'The girl who was stabbed? She'll be all right,' the doctor said. 'Lost a lot of blood, but I think we got there just in time.' He was fishing in his bag. 'I'm going to put your wrist in a splint, my dear, but it's very swollen just now. The bandages will need to be changed tomorrow.'

145

The policeman had his notebook open. 'I shall want a full statement, miss,' he said.

'Not just now,' said Miss Martin firmly. 'Wait till she's feeling better.' She brought a kettle to the fire, and Tom reached for it and set it over the flames. His eyes met Lucy's and he smiled.

'It's going to be all right,' he said.

12

It was a frightening journey. The coach bumped and rattled over the rutted roads and Lucy sat in the musty-smelling darkness, nursing her splinted wrist and worrying about Daisy. The girl's stained, dirty dress would not meet over the bulky bandages that covered her chest and shoulders, and blood was already seeping through the dressings. Each jolt seemed to make the bleeding worse, and Lucy leaned forward to watch her fluttering breaths, terrified that each one would be her last. Cavendish rode beside the coach, occasionally leaning to look in through its window, but there would be no stopping until they came to the house.

At last the horses crunched across the gravel drive and stopped. Cavendish dismounted and opened the door of the coach. Behind him, Lucy could see people running down the steps from the house. A white apron gleamed in a lantern's glow, and in the next moment Bess was looking in beside her master.

'Oh, my goodness,' she said. 'Let's get these girls inside, quickly.'

Cavendish helped Lucy out, then held up his hand as Walter came forward. 'The other girl can't walk,' he said. 'Fetch a hurdle.'

A stable-boy was throwing rugs over the steaming coach-horses. 'Yes, sir. I'll take Captain.' He ran off, leading Cavendish's horse.

'Come along in, my dear,' said Bess, with a hand on

Lucy's arm. 'Such goings-on—I don't know what the world's coming to.'

Lucy looked back from the top of the steps, and saw Walter lift Daisy out of the coach and lay her carefully on a willow fencing hurdle. The stable boy covered her with a blanket, then he and Walter carried her into the house.

'Upstairs,' Bess directed them. 'She'll be in the blue room at the back.'

Daisy raised her hand a little as the men carried her past, and Lucy was immensely relieved to see she was still alive.

'Can I go with her?' she asked.

The housekeeper looked disapproving. 'You need to get to bed yourself,' she said. 'Just look at you, like something the cat brought in. What have you done to your wrist?'

Lucy ignored the question. 'But she's my friend,' she pleaded. Daisy had risked her life to tell Tom where the gang was hiding—and besides, Lucy felt a real warmth for the thin, yellow-haired girl who didn't complain although her life was so hard.

'Up to you, my dear,' said Bess. 'I dare say the poor soul will be glad of your company.'

She led the way into a warm bedroom where a fire burned in the grate and an oil lamp cast its radiance over the flowered wallpaper. 'Wait a moment,' she told the men who were holding the makeshift stretcher and its burden. 'I'll just put a sheet over that bed-cover.'

Lucy could see why. As Walter and the stable-boy carefully transferred Daisy onto the bed, she thought what a terrible object the girl looked in the clean, cosy room. Her hair was matted and dirty, and her filthy, bloodstained dress made a dreadful contrast to the freshly laundered sheet that Bess had thrown over the bed. It seemed as if a piece of the fierce, rough world belonging to the kitchen

148

people had intruded into this gracious house, a foreign object that did not belong here. *I could have been like that*, Lucy thought. A few more weeks in the company of the gang, and she would have started to forget how to be polite and clean and take a pride in behaving like a properly brought-up young lady. Even in the short time she had spent with the Duke and Ada, she had become ruder and more inclined to argue back. With them, when she had held her tongue, it was not for the sake of manners.

'I'll get some hot water,' said Bess. 'She'll need a good wash.' And she bustled away.

Lucy stared at Daisy's white face and remembered what she had said in the kitchen. *It's just luck*. And Lucy might so easily have been unlucky, like this girl. Wanting to do something to help, she began to tug with her good hand at the laces of the broken and shabby boots.

Daisy's dry lips moved. 'Lucy?'

'Yes, it's me,' Lucy said. 'You're safe here, it's all right.' She eased off first one boot then the other, and put them on the floor. Then she took Daisy's filthy hand in her own equally dirty one, and felt how the fingers, weak but determined, closed round hers.

An old memory stirred as Lucy watched the housekeeper's plump hands washing Daisy's thin limbs and drying them with a warm towel. Hadn't there been a nurse once who smelt of milk and sweet biscuits and whose lap was always a safe refuge? But she was long gone, and since then, the servants in Papa's house had become less friendly, exchanging their work grudgingly for the unreliable money he paid them. It had seemed an inevitable part of growing up that life should become more dry and hard. But now, as Bess took a clean flannel nightgown from where it hung on the fireguard and slipped it over Daisy's head, Lucy suddenly wanted to weep.

* * *

'Time to wake up.'

I must light the stove, Lucy thought. She pushed the bed-clothes back, still half in a dream of Ada and the cold kitchen, but it was Bess who stood there.

'No need to rush,' Bess said. 'But the master's going into town, and he'll want you with him. What would you like for breakfast? A nice boiled egg?'

'That would be lovely.'

'I brought you these clothes.' She laid a dress and a shawl on the bed, with a cotton petticoat. 'Could be a bit big, but we can't have you running round London dressed as a boy. Come down to the dining room when you're ready.'

'Yes,' said Lucy. 'Thank you.'

Cavendish was eating a kipper. He looked up, wiping his mouth with a napkin, and made no comment about Lucy's bruised face or the vast dress with its sleeves rolled up. 'Good morning,' he said. 'I trust you slept well?'

'Yes, thank you.' The soft bed had been wonderful.

'How is your wrist?'

'It's all right, thank you,' Lucy said politely, though the throbbing seemed even worse this morning. 'Bess put a new bandage on.'

'Your friend seems improved,' Cavendish said. 'I had a word with her this morning.'

'Oh, good,' said Lucy. After a pause, she added, 'It wasn't her fault. She didn't mean to get mixed up with them.'

Cavendish sighed. 'People seldom do,' he said. 'I've found that to be true, in a lifetime of criminal law. Very few wrong-doers ever tell you they meant it. Most of them hoped there would be something better in their lives,

150

something decent. Crime is so often the business of the disappointed.'

Lucy nodded, not knowing if she was expected to say anything.

'Walter will be at the door with the coach in half an hour,' Cavendish went on. 'I'll want you to tell your story to a colleague of mine.'

Lucy nodded again. And Bess brought her boiled egg, in a crocheted blue cosy to keep it warm.

The coach pulled up at an office not far from Lucy's house. 'Albert Apps used to work here,' Cavendish said as they walked up the steps.

Lucy, busy trying to hold the over-large dress clear of her feet, glanced at him but didn't answer. *Poor Albert*, she thought. He had gone in through this black-painted front door every day, and it was too late now to wonder whether he found any pleasure in the hours spent here. His days of getting up and going to work and cooking kippers and complaining about the flute were ended, and perhaps there was nobody to think them worth remembering.

A woman in a black dress opened the door and showed Cavendish and Lucy into a waiting room. She was suffering from a bad cold, and mopped at her nose with a small and sodden handkerchief. 'Please sid down,' she said, 'I'll ged Mr Brisket.'

Brisket, Lucy thought. *Of course*. The young man called William Jinks had been sent by Mr Brisket to find out why Albert had not come to work.

The woman came back with a short, round-faced man as compact and bouncy as a rubber ball. He shook hands vigorously with Cavendish and said, 'So what brings you here, George?'

'Quite a lot,' said Cavendish grimly.

151

Brisket's eyebrows went up. 'In that case,' he said, 'you had better come in.'

Lucy had thought they were already in, but the lawyer led them along a corridor and into a chilly, fireless back room where clerks sat hunched on high stools at a long desk, writing in thick ledgers. She saw William Jinks among them. He looked up for a moment and gave her a polite nod, then dipped his pen again and resumed his work.

At the far end of this room, Brisket opened a further door into his private, thick-carpeted office, which by contrast was so hot as to be almost stifling. Heavy curtains at the windows muffled the sounds of the street outside, and brown leather armchairs gleamed like chestnuts in the heat of a roaring fire.

'Sit down, sit down,' said Brisket, casting a faintly puzzled glance at Lucy's voluminous dress. 'I am all ears.'

The two lawyers talked to each other in a leisured way, over glasses of sherry. Lucy tried to pay attention, but she was soon deeply bored. Their long words were difficult to understand, and although she knew the discussion was important, she longed to be out of the stuffy room, doing something more active. In a strange way, she missed the hard, frightening days that were now ended. She had hated and feared the people she was mixed up with, but the danger and watchfulness and the sense of being in the real, hard world had brought a kind of excitement. Now that Finn had been rescued, the big task was to get her father released from prison, and sitting in the hot leather depths of this armchair seemed no way to go about it.

Mr Brisket's voice broke into her thoughts. 'Miss Bellman, can you tell us in your own words what events have occurred since your father was imprisoned?'

'I don't know where to start,' said Lucy in confusion, but this didn't seem to surprise him.

152

'On the night when Albert Apps was found dead—you remained in the house?'

'Yes.'

'And the next day?'

'I was still there—I had to help Ada.'

'Doing what?'

Brisket was writing her words down. It all took a very long time.

They stopped at a tavern for lunch. Walter was told to water the horses at a livery stable and get himself something to eat, and Lucy found herself escorted into a warm room with oak beams and a blazing fire. Cavendish ordered lamb chops and a bottle of claret, 'With cordial for the young lady.' She wondered if she could ask him to cut the meat up for her, as the splint on her wrist extended over her hand and prevented her from holding a fork, but he solved the problem without fuss. 'Use your fingers,' he told her. 'It's perfectly acceptable.' And Lucy was glad to obey, being ravenously hungry.

'Well, my dear,' he said when they had finished eating. 'We are making progress. The case against your father for the murder of Apps is certainly not sustainable. Your friend's evidence makes that clear.'

For a moment, Lucy didn't know what he meant, but he smiled at her puzzled face and explained. 'Daisy told me this morning of the plans she overheard. Her evidence proves that there was a definite intention by this man called the Duke to bring about Apps's death.'

Lucy almost clapped her hands with relief, but the splint and bandages warned her not to. 'So will Papa be free?' she asked.

'Possibly,' said Cavendish. 'But, of course, there are other considerations, as you know.'

153

He means the debts.

Perhaps she should not have told him about her father's gambling, but last night after the doctor had gone and they were waiting for Walter to come back with the carriage, there had been nothing to do but answer questions. And they were so cleverly put that one explanation had led inevitably to another.

'Some treacle pudding?' enquired Cavendish.

Lucy gazed at him, not sure what she should say. She had just eaten two lamb chops with mashed potato, but after the days of hard work and short rations, she was enchanted by the thought of more delicious food. Cavendish smiled again, and held up a finger to the waiter.

Despite the jolting rattle of the coach wheels over cobblestones, Lucy fell asleep on the upholstered seat, lulled by the warm dinner inside her and still very tired after the previous night's adventure. She woke as cold air blew in through the open door, and found they had stopped outside Miss Martin's school.

The girls were coming out, chattering among themselves, waving their white-gloved hands to friends as they set out for their various homes, escorted by servants. Lucy stared furtively through the glass, recognizing Betty Tucker and Emily Goole, Marion Bates and Christine Walters, but none of them even saw the girl with the bruised face who sat inside the coach.

Cavendish did not help Lucy out until the last of the pupils had gone round the corner, and she was grateful to him for that. She felt stiff and bruised as she stood beside him, pulling her shawl round her neck in the chill wind. Then Miss Martin was coming towards them, smiling.

She ushered them into her private sitting room, and Lucy stared enviously at the books that filled shelves on

154

the wall and at the tabby cat drowsing before the fire. *One day*, she thought, *I will have a room like this. If I can.*

Cavendish did not sit down. 'I'd be most grateful if I could leave this young lady in your care for a short while,' he said to Miss Martin. 'I have another visit to make.'

The teacher did not seem surprised. 'It will be a pleasure. It's very good of you to take so much trouble.'

'Not at all,' said Cavendish. 'One of these days,' he went on, 'we may have a police force which interests itself in identifying the guilty and protecting the innocent, but that is yet to come. They content themselves with arresting those villains from the lower classes whom they catch in the act, but for the larger questions of justice, those of us concerned with the law have to do what we can.'

'I wish there were more who felt as you do,' said Miss Martin. 'Polly, this gentleman has other business to attend to. Will you show him out?'

A housemaid who seemed hardly older than Lucy gave a little bob and said, 'Yes, M'm.'

When Cavendish had gone, Lucy asked, 'Is Tom here?'

'He is, indeed,' Miss Martin said. 'He and Finn are in the kitchen—they insisted on polishing all my silver for me.'

'And is Finn all right?'

'I hope so. He's very weak and thin, after what he's been through. But he has great spirit. Now,' the teacher added, 'we'll have some tea.'

Cups and saucers stood ready on a low table, and a kettle steamed gently on a trivet over the fire.

'It's wonderful to be here,' Lucy said, accepting a biscuit. 'I can't believe it's true.'

Miss Martin smiled at her, but said nothing. When they reached the stage of a second cup, she asked, 'Have you thought at all about the future, my dear?'

Lucy wasn't sure what she meant. 'I keep thinking about Papa,' she said. 'That's the most important thing.'

'Of course,' Miss Martin agreed. 'And I am sure Mr Cavendish has the matter in hand. But what about you, Lucy? Forgive me if I intrude into things that are none of my business, but if I understand the situation rightly, you are going to need some form of income of your own.'

'Yes.' Lucy stared down at the pale tea in the rose-painted cup. Her teacher knew why she had left the school. Probably everyone knew. 'It's not Papa's fault,' she said. 'It's just that he—'

'I do understand. But I was wondering—would you like to work here, as my assistant?'

'Oh!' Lucy gave a cry of delight, and the tea almost spilled. 'It's what I'd always hoped for!'

The teacher smiled. 'Should you need to live in,' she went on, 'there is a small room available upstairs. But we'll see.'

When Lucy had finished her tea, Miss Martin stood up. 'Now, my dear, I really think you should rest for a while. It was very late last night before we all got home, and I expect your wrist is painful.'

Lucy had been trying to ignore the throbbing ache, but she nodded and said, 'A bit.'

She followed Miss Martin upstairs to a pretty room with white-painted furniture and small forget-me-nots on the wallpaper. She thought she was far too excited to rest, but she obediently pushed off her boots and lay down. Within a few moments, she was asleep.

There were voices downstairs. For a moment, Lucy thought she was back in the old house, and sat up quickly in fear that Ada would shout at her. Then she leaned back against the pillows in relief.

156

There was a tap at her door, and the housemaid called Polly put her head in. 'Miss Martin says to tell you the gentlemen are back,' she said. 'They're in the sitting room, if you're wanting to come down.'

'Thank you,' said Lucy. *Gentlemen?* What did she mean? Cavendish and . . . who? A wild hope arose, but she dared not think it possible. She swung her feet to the floor and stooped to tug at a bootlace with her good hand. 'I'll come at once.'

'Shall I help you with that, miss?' Polly offered.

'Oh, yes, please.' Lucy sat back gratefully. Only last night, she herself had been trying to undo the laces of Daisy's boots. She would never again take the service of another person for granted.

'Ah, there you are,' said Cavendish—but Lucy hardly heard him. She was staring at the stoop-shouldered man who turned from the window, as if he was a magical, well-known stranger.

'Papa,' she whispered.

'Oh, my dear. Look at you.' His face crumpled a little as he took in Lucy's splinted wrist, her bruised face, and grotesquely large dress, then he held out his arms.

After a few moments, Cavendish cleared his throat and said, 'I have one piece of news which may be of interest to you, Lucy, macabre though it is. The body of a man was retrieved from the river this morning. It appears to fit your description of the person known as the Duke.'

Lucy turned to him from her father's embrace, wide-eyed with relief as the dripping ghost receded from her secret mind. There was no fear now that the Duke waited for her in the dark streets, ready to step from some doorway and put his hand on her shoulder. And yet—she thought of him standing at a coffee stall, telling his wild stories as he munched untidily at a meat pie, and knew her memory of him would have an odd trace of sadness mixed with the horror. When a man died, all his hopes and his pride, no matter how mad, died with him.

'I am sure Mr Cavendish has a lot more to tell you,' Miss Martin said, 'but if you will forgive me, I have some things to attend to.' She left them together in the room.

Lucy, sitting on a low footstool by her father's chair, could hardly take in the meaning of what the lawyer was saying as he began a detailed statement.

Jeremy seemed equally baffled as the measured flow of words went on. Then he asked, 'You mean the house is still legally mine?' He sounded dazed.

'So it seems,' said Cavendish. 'My colleague, Mr Brisket, has been investigating the case on behalf of his deceased employee, Albert Apps, who had a tenancy agreement with you. Had Winterthorn's claim to be the rightful owner of the house been substantiated, it would of course have rendered the tenancy invalid, but he can find no trace of a written mortgage document. Do you remember signing any such thing?'

'Well, no,' Jeremy admitted. 'I've never been much of a one for paperwork. He said he would see to all that.'

Cavendish sighed. 'And payments were in cash, I suppose?'

'Yes. He said it was more convenient.'

'I have no doubt it was,' Cavendish said drily. 'However, it does seem that the house remains your property. And in that case, it can be used as security to raise funds for the payment of creditors. I could undertake those arrangements, if you wish.' He glanced at Lucy with a slight frown. 'Perhaps you should leave us to talk business, my dear. I am sure this is very boring for you.'

Lucy half got up, but her father took her good hand gently. 'My daughter has earned the right to know about

158

things that concern us both,' he said. 'Without her, I tremble to think what would have happened. And . . . she is aware of my weaknesses, which I will try my best to conquer.' He did not look at her, but his warm grasp tightened a little. Then he sat back.

'I would be more than grateful if you will act for me,' he told Cavendish. 'I have never been good at the business of earning and spending, I can see that now. I have made many mistakes. And we must not delude ourselves—I am likely to make many more. There need to be some changes.' He felt in the inside pocket of his jacket and produced an envelope, then turned to Lucy. 'Your grandmother wrote to me,' he said. 'You'll know why.'

He unfolded the letter, and Lucy bit her lip. Had she done wrong in telling her grandma about Papa being in prison?

'Living in Exeter has not entirely suited her,' Jeremy said. 'It's comfortable enough, but she misses her busy days of running the inn. She would rather be in London, she says, where there's more life. So she proposes to come and be my housekeeper.'

Lucy found herself laughing with sheer delight. 'Oh, that's wonderful!' She saw exactly what her grandmother planned to do. Living in the same house, she would manage the money and make sure bills were paid. But . . . where was the money to come from?

Cavendish was looking cautious. 'Bear in mind that the house is not what it was when you lived there,' he said to Jeremy. 'You'll remember it was completely stripped of its contents when you lost control of it.'

Lucy's father put a hand to his head as if in confusion. 'Yes, of course—I was forgetting.' Then he took a sharp breath. 'What happened to my flute? It was up in that poky bedroom.'

'I put it with my things,' said Lucy. 'It's under my bed.' Anxiety swept over her.

'It will probably still be there,' said Cavendish. 'I see no reason why not. The house has of course been shut up since Winterthorn's death—the police saw to that.' He looked at Jeremy carefully. 'Would you propose to go on running the shop?'

'I suppose so.' Lucy's father shrugged. 'What else can I do? Besides, it's a job for Tom.'

'If you will forgive me,' said Cavendish, 'I must tell you that the shop is a complete waste of your time. Old clothes will never make enough to keep a household running in any decent style.'

'Then what am I to do?' Lucy was glad to see that her father looked irritable rather than dejected. He was starting to find his energy again.

Cavendish put his fingers together and gazed at the ceiling. 'It so happens that I know of a very pleasant small tavern in Shepherd's Bush. It has a regular clientele—respectable local people. Ample living accommodation and a good kitchen garden at the back. And the tenants have just retired.' He met Jeremy's eye. 'Your mother-in-law, I gather, is experienced in the licensed trade business?'

'She's been in it all her life.' Lucy's father sounded almost breathless.

Cavendish nodded thoughtfully. 'With a word from me,' he said, 'I think the tenancy could be secured, on the understanding that this lady, Mrs—?'

'Ash,' said Jeremy.

'That Mrs Ash must be the licensee. She would need your help, of course, but she would be responsible for the running of the business. Young Tom could learn the trade and make himself useful,' Cavendish added. 'He's a strong boy, very capable.'

'And Finn could help,' Lucy said eagerly. 'There are lots of things he can do!' Then she remembered her own good news. 'Papa, Miss Martin has asked me to be her assistant! Isn't it wonderful? I can live here, there's a lovely little room upstairs. But I'll come and see you often,' she added quickly, 'and Grandma will tell the bees!'

'Bees?' Her father put his hand to his forehead, astonished. 'And you are going to be—a *teacher*?'

'I'll go on learning, too!' Lucy told him, excited by the thought of the books waiting on their shelves.

'Heavens,' said Jeremy. 'It seems no time since you were a baby. I never thought I'd lose you so soon.'

Lucy kissed him. 'Papa, you'll never lose me,' she said.

Miss Martin came into the room. 'I am sure you gentlemen would like a glass of sherry,' she said, then turned to Lucy. 'Tom is dying to see you. Will you go and talk to him? He's upstairs with Finn, in the room next to the one you were in.'

'Oh, *yes*,' said Lucy. And she gathered up the skirts of her huge dress and ran.

Tom grinned at the sight of her. 'Who on earth gave you that?' he said. 'We used to sell better stuff in the shop.'

Finn was in one of the two beds in the pink-curtained room with its sloping ceiling, and he held out his arms to Lucy. She sat down and hugged him, and tears pricked her eyes as she remembered the desperate moments outside the cellar door.

'You rescued me,' said Finn.

'Proper heroine, isn't she,' said Tom. He looked at Lucy and shook his head. 'I can't believe you came over the roof.'

'Well, I did,' said Lucy. She could hardly believe it herself

161

now. 'And everything's coming right. Papa's downstairs with Mr Cavendish, and I'm going to work here as a pupil teacher, and Grandma's coming back from Exeter. She's going to run an inn again, and you're going to help her, with Papa! If you want to, that is. I hope you will.'

The boys listened in astonishment.

'Talk about luck,' Tom said. 'The Duke didn't know what he was doing, did he, when he picked old Cavendish's house to rob. *And* took you with him. Two big mistakes.'

'I suppose so,' said Lucy. Then she added, 'You know the Duke's—'

Tom nodded. 'Yes, I heard. And Slip, too. I went to get some shopping for Miss Martin this morning, and they were all talking about it in the market.'

I dealt with Slip. The Duke's drunken voice sounded again in Lucy's mind. She shuddered, but she was full of an awful curiosity. 'What happened to him?'

'They found him in the ditch, when the tide went out. With his throat cut.'

'Horrible.' She brooded for a moment. 'And what about Ada and the others? I wonder where they got to.'

'They ran away,' said Finn. 'I heard them. The Duke was shouting and roaring, and things were banging about, and everyone was running. Then they were all gone.'

'Except poor Daisy,' said Lucy.

Tom looked up quickly. 'Is she going to be all right?'

'Yes, I think so. Mr Cavendish was talking to her this morning. And when we were in the coach, he said he'd find her a job as a housemaid when she's better. He knows lots of people with big houses.'

'I'll go and see her,' said Tom. 'We'd have had no chance without Daisy. She made it all possible.'

Finn turned on his side. His eyelids were closing. Lucy pulled the covers round him gently, and she and Tom sat

162

watching him as his breathing deepened and he drifted into sleep.

'It feels so safe,' Lucy said, quietly so as not to wake the little boy. 'But it isn't really. There are always people out there like the Duke.'

'Nothing's safe,' said Tom. 'But it's all right. As long as you're lucky.'

Lucy nodded slowly. Her father believed in luck, too, and look what that had led to. But then, his idea of good fortune had always been riches, and Tom meant something else.

As if to confirm her understanding, Tom said, *'We're* lucky, aren't we?' His thin face glowed as he looked round the room. 'I think we always will be.' He reached for her good hand and held it, and Lucy smiled as her worries fell away. There would be more, but they could be overcome.

'Yes,' she said. 'We will.'

Also by Alison Prince

Oranges and Murder
ISBN 0 19 275264 2

Winner of the Scottish Arts Council Children's Book of the Year Award, 2002

'Lord James. Called after your old man, weren't you?'

Joey has always known that Curly the coster isn't his real father, but he can't believe that he is the son of a lord as the other boys say. Anyway, he's too busy to think about it much. He's planning to set up on his own as a market trader, and he dreams of a red-haired girl called Annie.

But when he meets Quill Quennell, the screever, a man who will write letters for anyone who can pay, and who seems to know something about Joey's past, Joey begins to wonder if there is something in the gossip after all. Then Quennell is murdered and Joey has to go into hiding, afraid for his own life. If the screever was killed to keep him quiet, what was the secret he knew? And can Joey find out the truth before it is too late?

'Prince's London is alive with colour in both character and setting . . . The plot twists and turns with absolute veracity . . . '
Books for Keeps

'Absorbing, atmospheric and meticulously researched'
Shelf Life

'Set in Victorian London, this is a wonderfully atmospheric tale of murder and intrigue'
Booktrusted News

Other Oxford historical novels

Stella
Catherine R. Johnson
ISBN 0 19 275231 6

There was a scream from the back of the stalls. 'She's dead! There's a woman here dead!' And suddenly the heavy red velvet curtains swung shut.

Stella's stage career as 'The incomparable Stella Morisco' comes to an abrupt end with the death of her guardian, Nana. How can Stella carry on with her clairvoyance and seances without Nana to pick out the punters and give her tips on what to say to them? But she has to earn a living somehow and working in the music halls is all Stella has ever known. And, after all, it is just pretend, isn't it? It doesn't do any harm.

But then Stella begins to see things: a thin, haggard looking clergyman, an African woman in a bright robe, and a young boy who drowned years ago. What have they to do with her? Why have they come into her life now? Together with Thomas, the drowned boy's brother, Stella tries to make sense of it all and rebuild her life without Nana.

Stop the Train
Geraldine McCaughrean
ISBN 0 19 275266 9

*' . . . there will be no Florence Station on the Red Rock Railroad Line . . .
From here on out the trains won't be stopping at Florence. Ever.'*

Cissy and her family are among the first settlers to make their
homes in the new town of Florence, Oklahoma in the 1890s. The
trouble is, the railroad company wants the land for itself, and when
the settlers refuse to sell their claims the railroad boss swears the
train will never stop in Florence again. Without the railroad the
town can't survive and the settlers try every means they can think
of to get the train to stop. But the railroad company always seems
one step ahead. Can there be a traitor in their midst? And will they
be able to force the train to a standstill before they all have to
abandon their new homes for ever? Cissy, her friends, family, and
neighbours resolve to stop the train, come what may—by fair
means or foul.

The Hidden Hand
Roger J. Green
ISBN 0 19 271916 5

Every night at midnight a silent, hidden hand turned up the lights in her brain. In her mind was a vast gallery, an art gallery with a single exhibit at the centre where her mind's eye could not possibly avoid it . . . She had to read the stark words . . . SALLY CLAY—WANTED FOR MURDER.

Sally hates her job as a maid at isolated North Grange and she hates her employer, the sadistic Noah North, even more. The only things that make her life worthwhile are her friendship with Hilda, Noah's daughter, and her love for Paul, the gardener.

And then, on one of the worst nights of the year, with a storm raging outside, she finds she has, quite by accident, Noah North's life within her power. Sally has to decide whether Noah North will live or die. It will be a decision that will overshadow and determine the rest of her life. Alone, on a fearful night of wind and rain, with her whole world collapsing around her, Sally makes her courageous decisions.